Fighting Fate
Sporting Pride #3
Charity Parkerson

Punk & Sissy Publications

Copyright

—Warning: This book is intended for readers over the age of 18. Some of my books contain allusions to past abuse and trauma.

Cover art: Temptation Creations

Editor: BZ Hercules & Consultants

Contents

Introduction

*FOR YEARS, NOTHING HAS **mattered except Chipper's career. Meeting Baylor has made him rethink everything. Baylor doesn't care.***

As one of the most sought-after wedding planners, Baylor is so busy traveling the world, he doesn't even have a home. Years ago, he stuffed his things in storage and simply stayed wherever his latest job took him. Since he mostly works with celebrities and the top one percent, he's learned to spot the men who are full of it and steer clear. He doesn't have time for a relationship anyhow.

Chipper isn't special, as much as he'd love to think he is.

Maybe Chipper has seen a lot of beds that aren't his, but he's an MMA champion. Having whoever he wants is a perk of the job. No one he's ever met is as immune to his charms as Baylor. Chipper has wanted no one as badly. Baylor thinks he isn't interested, but Chipper is no quitter. He got where he is by sheer determination and refusing to back down. He's not afraid to fight for what he wants, and Baylor is the one.

Fighting Fate is the third book in Charity Parkerson's Sporting Pride series. These are sports related romances, following men who find love while navigating high-profile careers. These are best enjoyed when read in order.

Author Note

THIS BOOK HAS CONTENT that could cause possible triggers. Please go to the content warning after the About Author page to read more. I do things this way so the people who need a warning get one, but the content isn't spoiled for people who don't need a warning. Thank you for your understanding.

Chapter One

EITHER CHIPPER BROWN KNEW everyone on the planet, or the guy was stalking him. Baylor leaned toward the second. This was the fifteenth wedding in a row with Chipper as a guest. As the MMA light heavyweight champion, the guy likely knew a ton of celebrities. But Baylor didn't recall seeing him before a year ago and he hadn't stopped popping up everywhere since.

Baylor had been the wedding planner for the stars for nearly five years. His career had skyrocketed after the first big party he put together and hadn't stopped since. It was all thanks to his best friend Bandit. In high school, they had been inseparable. Then Bandit had gotten picked up by a professional soccer team, and being Bandit, he hadn't left Baylor behind. Baylor had always had an eye for decor, and a knack for organizing while keeping people in line. When one of Bandit's teammates had mentioned wanting to put together a huge party for his son's first birthday, Bandit had shoved Baylor in his path. The next thing Baylor knew, life had taken a huge turn, and he had so many clients, he barely kept up. Sometimes, it was lonely. It was always exhausting. That didn't mean he needed a man like Chipper.

Chipper was everything a person would expect from a champion. He was perfectly sculpted and moved like a lion. The guy also had the most beautiful light brown eyes Baylor had ever seen, framed by long, dark lashes. He was also cocky, grating, and obviously thought the entire world revolved around his dick. Baylor wasn't unaware God had favorites. That didn't mean he would fall to his knees.

Tonight, Baylor felt the last five years of not sitting still. The backs of his eyes ached. An invisible weight seemed to sit on his shoulders and chest. He prayed he wasn't getting sick because he did not have time for that bullshit. As always, he bustled from one place to the next, ensuring his client's wedding went smoothly and stress free... for them. Baylor had five hundred guests to keep in line. He had to take a break.

His gaze slid across the reception hall. Everyone danced and drank. Things were winding down. The happy couple had already left for the night and the stragglers would be kicked out by staff at the end of the night. Then a cleaning crew would take care of the rest. The rental company for the decorations would pick up everything in the morning from the venue. Baylor's job was complete. His shoulders relaxed.

A pain bloomed behind his left eye. Baylor headed for the door. He needed the night air to clear his head. It was the perfect temperature in Southern California. Thankfully, since this was his favorite place to work, he did most weddings here. The majority of his clients lived in California and didn't have time to deal with a huge wedding somewhere else. It was the athletes that kept him hopping all over the U.S. He didn't mind. Baylor had gotten to see the country. There was nothing back home except Bandit, and he was usually too busy for Baylor these days.

Baylor sucked in a deep breath. His skin itched. Tonight, something felt lacking.

There was an emptiness threatening to swallow him.

"Hello, beautiful."

Baylor jumped at Chipper's sudden appearance. Despite his surprise, he couldn't stop his eyes from rolling. "Is there anyone you don't think is beautiful?"

An unrepentant and sigh-worthy smile stretched Chipper's lips. His expression quickly turned thoughtful. He scratched his chin. "Maybe mean people."

"So you just lied to me a second ago, then?"

Chipper laughed. "You're not mean. I think you're just shy."

Baylor scoffed. "I'm definitely not shy."

"Well, you're actually speaking to me tonight."

"You're a customer now," Baylor shot back, refusing to let Chipper's fat head grow. Chipper had hired him to throw a surprise birthday party for a friend. They hadn't worked out all the details yet. Mostly because of Baylor dodging him. He couldn't do that forever, though. Baylor couldn't damage his reputation just because Chipper made him crazy.

"Since you brought it up." Chipper's expression screamed Baylor had fallen into his trap.

Baylor opened his mouth to make more excuses about why they hadn't met to discuss things. His head spun so hard and fast, his arm shot out, seeking purchase. There was nothing there.

Then Chipper caught him. "Whoa. Are you okay? You're looking kind of pale."

Baylor cleared his throat and tried to straighten. "I just need to eat, I'm sure."

Chipper's concern didn't ebb. His gaze moved over Baylor's face. At least Baylor thought it did. Everything kept spinning. "Nah. That's not it. You're burning up." Chipper touched Baylor's forehead with the back of his hand. Baylor wanted to move from Chipper's arms, but his body wouldn't obey.

"You definitely have a fever. When was the last time you took a break?"

Baylor tried to think. Chills set in, making his teeth chatter. His knees weakened.

"Holy shit." Chipper swept Baylor off his feet. "You need a fucking keeper."

Baylor felt like reality slowly slipped away. He couldn't even think clearly enough to argue.

"Someone should definitely fucking spank you and put you in timeout. You'll fucking kill yourself with the schedule you keep."

Baylor felt his body floating. The sky moved above him. Chipper stared straight ahead. He shuffled around, easily shifting Baylor's body from arm to arm. Then Baylor heard the chirp of a car alarm.

"I'd ask you where you're staying, but I won't risk you dying. No doubt you'd do something stupid the minute I left you alone—like try to go back to work. I don't understand why Bandit allows this."

That last bit spurred him enough to force a few words out. "No one allows me anything."

Chipper looked down. He looked a lot more worried than he had a minute ago. That couldn't be good. "You sound weak as hell. Don't worry, though. I'm an awesome nurse."

A groan tore through Baylor's mind as Chipper bent and buckled him into the passenger seat of a car. Even in his fading state, the car smelled expensive. The world became less and less in focus.

"What in the hell is wrong with me?" Baylor didn't get to hear if Chipper answered. The world went black.

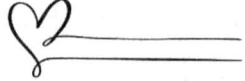

Was Chipper stalking Baylor? Yes. Had he ramped up his efforts in the last four-ish months? Also, yes. Was he embarrassed by his antics? That would be a yes too. Did he intend to stop? Probably not. The guy drove him insane. Chipper could have anyone in the world. He could pick up his phone right then, call absolutely anyone no matter their sex, and have them in his bed by the end of the night. Anyone. That wasn't conceit. It was reality.

The thing about all that bullshit was no one wanted him for him. Everyone wanted the world champion. They didn't care to know him for real. He doubted any of them knew anything about him beyond his stats or whatever. Baylor didn't want him. That had never happened to him before. Admittedly, and as cliche as it was, that had been what truly caught his attention at first. Beyond Baylor's looks, of course, because the guy was... damn. Dark hair, green eyes, and tiny body. He was an angry sprite. Chipper smiled. Yeah. That was what he liked. Baylor had gumption. He had a spark. The guy was a little mean, to be honest. *Le sigh*. He had Chipper fascinated. He also worked too damn much. Baylor was killing himself.

Chipper glanced Baylor's way as he drove home. He was out cold. Chipper fought the urge to run his fingers through Baylor's thick hair. It looked soft. He wasn't trying to get creepy, though. The stalking was bad enough. Baylor had been burning up when Chipper checked earlier. He needed to get him home and check for sure. To him, by touch, it felt like he had a really high fever. Chipper needed to know if this should be a trip to the ER.

His house came into view, and he let out a sigh of relief. Worry beat at his brain. He had always been an overthinker, and this was enough to send him over the edge. Illness was his kryptonite. He was ready to dance around Baylor like an old mother hen. Chipper hated this shit. He pulled into his garage and parked his Audi next to his truck. Chipper jumped from the vehicle and circled it to Baylor's side. He gently lifted him out and carried him inside. Baylor never budged. Chipper's anxiety shot through the roof. Not only did he not want anything bad to happen to Baylor, but he would also have a hell of a time explaining why he—the guy who had been stalking him—had Baylor's dead body in his house. That was a bad look.

He chose the spare room next door to his bedroom. There was a connecting door. Chipper could leave it open so he could keep an eye on him throughout the night. As he stepped into the room, Chipper froze. What if this was some sort of flu and Baylor choked on his own vomit or something in the night? Next door wasn't good enough. Anything could happen. He switched directions and carried Baylor to his bed. Chipper could keep a closer watch over him here.

After getting Baylor settled, Chipper stared at him for a moment. Shoes! Chipper removed the guy's shoes but left his socks. Then he immediately changed his mind and took off his socks too. Chipper hated sleeping in his socks. The guy had nice feet. Chipper wasn't like a foot guy or anything, but it was obvious Baylor found time to care for himself in some ways. He stepped back again. Baylor still wore his suit. Damn. It took some work, but he got the guy out of his jacket and tie. Then he realized he wouldn't want to sleep in a long sleeve dress shirt. The pants were probably uncomfortable too, but Chipper wouldn't go there. He would take off his belt, though. No one wanted to sleep in one of those. He could find Baylor some pajama pants. Chipper tossed out the idea. They were nowhere near the same size. Shit. Baylor had a cute body. Chipper tucked it beneath the covers before he turned into a full-on perv. He went in search of the thermometer.

It took Chipper a minute to find it. He never got sick. Seriously. Never. He had the immune system of a horse. Chipper headed back to the bedroom. At some point, Baylor had rolled onto his side and curled into a ball. He shivered, but was still asleep. Chipper scanned his forehead. The screen turned red and beeped loudly several times—like a blaring alarm. Chipper didn't know the thing did that. He checked the numbers. Fuck. One hundred and three point four. That sounded bad. Chipper tossed the thermometer on the nightstand and rushed back to the bathroom. He found his bathroom bottle of Tylenol, as opposed to kitchen Tylenol and car Tylenol. Oh, and his living room one. Wait. That was ibuprofen. He might need that too. Chipper hesitated. Which one was better for fever? Fuck it. This one was closer. He raced back into the bedroom and grabbed a bottle of water from the fridge in his room. Chipper needed to keep ice packs close after his matches. Plus, he was boujee. He could afford to be.

After cracking open the bottle and shaking out a couple of pills, he sat on the edge of the bed. Chipper ran his fingers through Baylor's hair. "Hey, gorgeous. I need you to take these pills. You have a really high fever."

Baylor's eyes peeked open a hair.

Chipper smiled. "Hi. There you are. Do you think you can sit up enough to take these?"

Baylor tried to sit up.

Chipper helped. He watched over him as Baylor swallowed the meds. It looked like they didn't want to go down. He was a little worried over Baylor's lack of fight. It wasn't like him to have anything to do with Chipper. Much less be in Chipper's bed. Baylor didn't even ask where he was.

"What else do you need? I can get it delivered."

"Everything hurts. Cold."

Chipper decided, since Baylor was awake enough to consent, now was a good time to get him comfortable. "They'd be huge on you, but would you like to borrow something else to wear? Someone gave me these thick flannel pajamas for Christmas. I never wear them. I'm too hot natured."

Baylor nodded. He looked ready to fall over.

"Come on." Chipper got him settled under the covers. "Rest. I'll grab them." He rushed around the room, hunting. By the time he found the outfit, Baylor was out of it again. Chipper hated to wake him, but he didn't know what else to do. "Hey. Here are those pajamas we talked about." He handed them to Baylor.

Baylor halfheartedly held them against his body. "Can't. Too tired."

Chipper shifted from foot to foot. "I could do it, but I don't want to make you feel uncomfortable. I'm pretty sure I already do that," Chipper muttered under his breath.

"Don't feel good enough to care."

Chipper smiled. Damn. The guy really was sick. Chipper rearranged his features and went to work. He tried to keep things impersonal and made a point of averting his eyes at a certain point. By the time he finished, Baylor shook so hard, Chipper wondered if he should call an ambulance.

"Do I need to call someone?"

Baylor's teeth chattered. "My assistant. I have appointments."

"Um. The fuck you do. You're not leaving this bed until you're better. Are you trying to fucking kill yourself?"

"Have to reschedule."

"For fuck's sake." He crawled into bed and pushed Baylor over so he could hold him. Chipper piled the covers on top of them. "Let's get you warm and then I'll take care of everything. I know your business is everything to you. Lord knows, I know it. But no one wants to meet with you while you're like this. Nobody wants to catch this shit. Do you want that on you? Do you want clients telling everyone you gave them the bionic flu or whatever?"

Baylor's teeth chattered. He buried his face against Chipper's chest. "The code to my phone is easy. It's nine one one zero zero one. My assistant's name is Sacha. There's one only contact on my phone under that name."

"I should hope so. How many Sacha's are in the world?"

Baylor might have been sick, but that didn't stop him from pinching him.

Chipper laughed. "Don't abuse me. I'll come."

Baylor chuckled. It was deep and sounded like it hurt. "We're still not friends."

Chipper couldn't stop smiling. "God, no. Who could like you?"

Baylor shook with silent laughter.

Without thinking, Chipper pressed his lips against Baylor's head. He didn't pull away. "Go to sleep. I've got you."

He did. Sick patient or not, it was nice to not be alone. There was no pressure to be on the whole time. He just got to enjoy the sound of someone else's breathing. Too many people took that for granted.

Chapter Two

BAYLOR HAD NO IDEA how much time passed. He woke up and went right back to sleep. Sometimes, Chipper was there, holding him. Others, he was alone, or Chipper tried pouring water down his throat. This time, light peeked through the gap in the curtains. He considered trying to get up, but his body just wouldn't budge. It was like he was paralyzed. Weakness owned him.

Chipper strolled into the room, moving like the fighter he was. Baylor couldn't explain that thought. He had simply met countless athletes over the years. Each sport seemed to have players developing a specific walk. Hell, maybe it was just confidence. He sat on the edge of the bed. "Hey. You're awake. You'll be happy to know, Sacha, who I expected to be a girl for whatever reason, is covering your appointments. According to Bandit, Sacha has been with you long enough to take care of your business until you're well. So you can chill and heal."

"You talked to Bandit?" Baylor couldn't explain why that tidbit soothed him. But if Bandit said everything was taken care of, then it would be. Bandit was the only person on earth who had never let him down. People were huge disappointments.

"Yes. He said to tell you to rest and get better because he would hate to have to come here and spank you in my presence."

Baylor rolled his eyes. "He would say that."

Chipper smirked. "I told him there was no need. I would spank you in his stead."

Thank god his body was half dead. Otherwise, he would've gone hard right then. Apparently, a man who took great care of him was his kink. Chipper had never looked sexier. In an attempt to hide his desire, Baylor released a loud, put-upon sigh. "Bed it is, I guess."

Chipper gave him a sharp nod and stood. He moved across the room. "For now, take something for the fever." He bent and grabbed water from a wine fridge. Baylor enjoyed the show. He came back and handed the bottle to Baylor before shaking out two ibuprofens. "I gave you Tylenol last, so take these."

Baylor accepted the pills. "When did I take Tylenol?"

Chipper glanced toward the clock. "A little over four hours ago."

"I don't even remember that."

A heart-stopping smile flashed his way. "I'm not surprised. You said I have pretty eyes."

He wanted to die.

"You'd never say that if you were fully awake."

Well, at least Chipper understood that.

"Anyhow. I need a shower. Sit tight and I'll bring you some soup when I get out."

Baylor's stomach churned. "That's okay. I don't think I can eat."

"I wasn't asking." Damn. That bossiness got him hot. Please let that be the fever. He couldn't keep finding things he liked about Chipper. "You're weak enough as it is. You'll never get better if you don't try to keep up your strength. Any allergies?"

Baylor knew he was sick because the question made him tear up. He cleared his throat. "Just sweet potatoes. Thank you." Fuck. No one would ever understand how badly he hated that Chipper was the one who showed up when he was at his worst.

Chipper winked and headed for the shower. Baylor watched him go with his heart in his throat. Why was he perfect? It had to be a ploy. No one except Bandit worried about him or cared about him. That was reality. He didn't know Chipper's game, but he knew it had to be just that: a game.

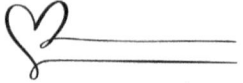

Chipper rushed through his shower, trying not to think about the way Baylor's eyes had filled with tears when he asked about allergies. He wished he could call Bandit back and ask him what in the hell that was about. Chipper doubted Bandit would spill. On the other hand, Bandit had been suspiciously relieved Chipper had taken Baylor in—almost as if he thought Baylor would simply fall over and die without him. Chipper had a bad feeling he would. First off, he had passed out in a parking lot. If Chipper hadn't been there, anything could have happened. He couldn't imagine how long Baylor had refused to acknowledge his symptoms before things came to that.

Baylor was so fucking stubborn. He would work himself to death.

He was slightly surprised to see Baylor still in bed when he left the bathroom. His eyes were closed, so Chipper sneaked past and headed for the kitchen. A bark of laughter escaped him when his gaze landed on the kitchen counter. Baylor's phone was gone. Chipper had plugged it up to charge. With a shake of his head, he grabbed the soup from the fridge he had ordered earlier. He popped it in the microwave. It didn't take long for him to have a tray ready to go. He tried to be quiet, hoping he would bust Baylor on his phone. Instead, he found him looking like he wanted to curl up and die.

"Don't worry. I ordered the soup. You don't want my cooking."

"I have a bad feeling I won't keep it down either way."

Chipper set the tray next to the bed. "It's okay. I'll take care of you no matter what happens. Now, hand it over."

The guilt that passed over Baylor's features was priceless. He still tried to act innocent. "What?"

Chipper wiggled his fingers in a silent demand to give up the phone.

With an eye roll, Baylor's arm appeared from the beneath the covers with the phone. "I didn't call anyone. I just wanted to check my emails."

"Mhmm." Chipper didn't believe it for a minute. He stuffed the device in his pocket. "Come on. Let's sit you up and get something in you." He smirked.

The innuendo earned him another eye roll. "How do you know I'm not a top?"

Chipper chuckled. He loved directness as much as playing. "I feel confident I could take it." He grabbed the bowl and spoon and sat on the edge of the bed. "Now, here comes the airplane."

The droll look he received made his ridiculous act worthwhile. "I can feed myself."

"Can you?" He held out the empty spoon. "Show me."

The spoon shook uncontrollably the moment Baylor touched it.

Chipper took it back. "That's what I thought." He dipped the spoon in the soup. "I've had this before. It's not bad." He scooped up some chicken along with the broth.

Baylor dutifully opened and wrapped his lips around the spoon.

Chipper was fascinated and hard. So fucking hard. God. He had never wanted anyone the way he did Baylor. Sick or not. Chipper couldn't explain it. There was something here. He just didn't know how to get Baylor to see it. There had to be a reason he kept rearranging his life for Baylor.

"I can't see you eating this. It seems too lightweight. I don't know what I'm trying to say. Hopefully, you know what I mean."

Chipper nodded. "You've obviously never gotten your teeth knocked down your throat. Soup is all that's going down after that."

"Actually, I have."

The rage struck hard and fast, forcing Chipper to take a steadying breath. "Who?" It was all Chipper could manage.

A sad smile passed over Baylor's lips. "It doesn't matter." He managed a few more bites before the shaking set in again. "I have to stop."

Chipper set the bowl aside. He didn't like the way Baylor didn't seem to be getting any better. "Do I need to take you to a doctor or the ER or something?"

Baylor shook his head. "I'm just tired." His teeth chattered. "And cold."

"Do I need to share my warmth again?" Chipper fought hard to hide his hope.

Baylor must have felt terrible because he nodded. "If you don't mind?"

Chipper stood and helped Baylor scoot over. "Mind? I fucking love to cuddle. It doesn't happen often."

Despite the fact he seemed to be going downhill fast, Baylor kept the conversation going. "I don't believe that for a second."

After climbing beneath the covers, Chipper hauled Baylor into arms and used his size to warm as much of him as possible. "Why? Do I look like I cuddle complete strangers on the street or something?"

"It's not that," Baylor said against his chest. "I doubt your bed is ever empty. I'm probably cramping your style right now."

For a minute, Chipper stared at nothing over the top of Baylor's head before shaking off the disappointment. "Yeah. I suppose that's what everybody sees when they look at me."

Silence grew between them. He thought Baylor dozed. It startled him a little when Baylor spoke again. "I'm sorry. If anyone knows you shouldn't judge a book by its cover, it's me. You've been amazing. I don't know what would've happened to me if you hadn't been there."

Without thinking, Chipper kissed the top of Baylor's head. "Don't sweat it. It's not like I haven't earned that reputation. I just wish..." He didn't bother to finish. No one cared.

"What do you wish?" Baylor asked so quietly, it was like he tried not to spook Chipper.

He didn't know why, but Chipper found himself being honest. "I wish just one person would see me for real. I guess that's a lot to ask."

A light kiss brushed his neck.

Chipper closed his eyes and savored the sweet moment. It meant nothing. Baylor was sick and Chipper was his nurse. The guy would never want him. Several minutes passed. The shaking stopped. Baylor's breathing evened. Chipper closed his eyes and dreamed. He had no clue how much time passed before he felt Baylor's fingers sneak into his pocket.

"You'd better be reaching for my dick because I know you're not trying to get your phone."

Baylor huffed.

A huge grin split Chipper's face. This was the life he wanted. Obviously, in his dream, Baylor wasn't sick, but still. Holding Baylor like this and feeling this happiness in his chest, that was what he fought to find. His smile fell. He wished it wasn't temporary. His arms tightened around Baylor. It didn't matter. He would take what he could get. Happiness didn't find him often.

Chapter Three

IT TOOK EVERY OUNCE of Baylor's strength and willpower to roll from the bed. He had to find his phone, pray it wasn't dead, and see what he could do to keep from losing clients. He never thought he would be down this long, and he couldn't expect Sacha to do everything. Since he didn't see the device in the room, he went in search of Chipper. He made it to the bedroom door before tripping over the huge pants he wore. Baylor didn't have the energy for this. He let them hit the floor. The shirt he wore nearly came to his knees and covered everything, so what the fuck ever. He felt too bad to care.

Baylor followed a rhythmic sound alongside an upbeat metal song. He rounded the corner into an open doorway and froze. In nothing but shorts, Chipper bounced on his toes while punching and kicking a punching bag that hung from the ceiling. Sweat poured down the most perfect body Baylor had ever seen. He vaguely recalled cuddling against that solid body. Holy hell. Even on the edge of death, Baylor's body tingled. Chipper's entire body from the collarbone down was tattooed. Baylor couldn't tear his eyes away.

Since Chipper had his back to the doorway and looked busy, Baylor moved to a stack of nearby mats against the wall and sat. He leaned back, bracing his shoulder blades against the wall. The mats were long enough for him to stretch his legs out. He crossed his ankles and settled in. Baylor had no clue how long these workouts took, but he understood this was Chipper's job. Just like he wouldn't appreciate being interrupted while working, he would extend the same courtesy. His reluctance to bother Chipper had nothing to do with enjoying the show. Nothing at all.

By the time Chipper stopped abusing the bag, his shoulders heaved from the exertion. More sweat rolled down his back. He grabbed a nearby bottle of water and turned. Chipper jumped slightly at the sight of him.

"Hey. What are you doing out of bed?"

Fighting for his goddamn life. That's what he was doing. Holy motherfucking hell. Just abs. Obliques. The chest. He couldn't breathe. It wasn't fair. No one should look like him.

Chipper's brow furrowed. "Are you okay? You're sweating. I don't think you should be up." He moved as if to cross the room. As if a thought hit, he froze and changed directions. As Baylor looked on, he grabbed a towel and swiped the sweat from his torso and Baylor watched every second. Damn. He was thirsty. His mouth was the Sahara.

Chipper tossed the towel aside and headed his way. "Come on."

Before Baylor said a word or knew what would happen, Chipper easily swept him into his arms.

"Back to bed. I bet if I take your temperature, you'll still have a fever. Why did you get up?" He didn't give Baylor a chance to answer. It was as if he spoke to himself. "I guess I should've figured out a way for you to call for me so I could bring you whatever you need. Don't worry. I'll figure out something. One thing I know I can leave you a phone or you'll try to work."

"I need to work."

Chipper snorted. Even that was sexy. "See? Can't be trusted." He gently tucked Baylor back into bed. "Let's see." He sat on the edge and snagged a nearby thermometer. After a quick scan of his forehead, an alarm sounded. He turned the device Baylor's way so he could see. "One hundred and two. Don't get out of bed again until this has a green screen and has you at most ninety-nine. Understand?" He hesitated. "Unless you need to use the restroom, of course."

Even though he was about ninety percent sure he was dying, Baylor still argued. "You don't understand. I need to appease clients before they find someone else. I have two weddings next weekend."

"Stop." Chipper's tone was so stern. Baylor automatically went quiet. He eyed Baylor, as if ensuring he would zip it before speaking again. "I told you I'd take care of everything, and I have. Sacha has you. I have you."

He did. Baylor couldn't deny that. "I know. You've been amazing." Baylor regretted the admission immediately.

A huge grin lit Chipper's face. "You like me." He sang the words, making Baylor groan. It hurt his throat. "Ow."

Chipper turned serious, like a switch had been flipped. "What hurts?"

"My throat."

"I'll make you some honey tea."

There had to be a law against someone like Chipper existing. He made all the right moves and his name fit. Nothing seemed to bring him down. The only thing that soothed Baylor was the sound of his voice. "Is Chipper your real name?"

"It's Chip. My mom called me Chipper, and it stuck."

"Fits you."

Baylor watched Chipper's mouth lift in one corner. The smile had a hint of sadness to it. "She would've loved to hear it. Honey tea coming your way."

Baylor watched him walk away with a combination of affection and something else he couldn't place. Hope, maybe? He hadn't felt that pesky emotion for so long, he couldn't recall what it felt like. At a moment when he felt the absolute worse, Baylor teetered. He could give up now or he could fight. Baylor wasn't sure yet which he would choose. He had always thought he knew which way he would go.

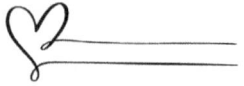

While the water heated, Chipper stared at nothing, seeing only the images in his mind. When he had started his chase, Chipper hadn't truly known what he sought. He had never been like this. While he was the type of guy who liked everyone and made friends everywhere he went, he wasn't so sure anymore Baylor's resistance was what spoke to him. Plenty of people hadn't meshed with him over the years. He had never acted like this. The mystery of it had him looking too hard at Baylor. What he saw terrified him a little. It was like Baylor wanted to die. His obsession with work wasn't normal. It was a rush toward the grave.

He poured Baylor a cup of tea and headed back to the bedroom. Baylor was out again.

He set the cup on the bedside table and made his way to the bathroom. He needed a shower and then he might hold Baylor again for a while. Truthfully, he needed to finish his workout. His next fight could go either way. He had to be in the best shape of his life. The thing about being a world champion meant no one reached challenger stage without being good enough to issue a challenge. He always had to assume there was a chance he would lose.

Chipper stood under the warm water and lost himself in thought. He liked Baylor. It was more than sexual attraction or a need to soothe his pride. The guy had mettle. He fought the urge to call Bandit and ask to hear more. But even though they were friends, Bandit was Baylor's best friend. He likely wouldn't tell Chipper anything too personal. A thought hit. He wondered if the two had ever been together. Chipper wouldn't be surprised. They had gone to high school together. Two gay boys with nothing but raging hormones had at least made out. Chipper didn't know why he couldn't stop obsessing.

"Swear I'm not looking."

The hurried words were followed by the sounds of retching.

Chipper jumped from the shower so fast, he almost fell. He snatched up the nearby towel and wrapped it around his waist before rushing to Baylor's side like he could throw up for him. Since there really wasn't anything in Baylor's stomach, he only dry heaved. It sounded like it hurt.

He fell against the wall next to the toilet when the heaving seemed to pass. "God. If I'm dying, this needs to go on and take me. I'll go willingly. There's no reason to torture me any longer."

The strange part was, Chipper got the feeling Baylor actually meant the speech for God. He sounded like he begged for mercy from the bottom of his soul. Chipper's throat swelled unexpectedly from the plea. He turned away. With the press of a few buttons, he had the tub filling with water at his usual temperature. He dumped some lavender bath salts in the water and then a bath bomb that would turn the water a milky white. Thankfully, the competing smells weren't overwhelming. He just wanted to ensure Baylor had his dignity while Chipper tried to help.

Thankfully, the computerized system filled the tub quickly and automatically stopped at the perfect depth. He moved back to Baylor's side. "Come on. A warm bath will help. I'll have to undress you, but I promise I'll be respectful."

Baylor didn't make a sound or protest as Chipper stripped him and set him in the tub. His lifelessness had Chipper nervously chatting. "I hope the temperature is okay. If not, I can turn it up or down. Either way, it'll stay that temp. I ordered this setup after a fight in Japan. Their technology is worlds ahead of ours. After fights, it's nice to soak forever and let the heat loosen my muscles. I don't know if it has the same results for illness, but it's worth a shot." When he realized he sounded like a panicked idiot, which probably helped nothing, he backed toward the door. "I'll leave you alone to bathe. I'll change the sheets and whatnot so you can come back to clean bedding. We'll beat this one way or another."

"Please stay."

The quietly spoken plea had Chipper leaping to sit next to the tub. He stared at Baylor's defeated expression. "Whatever you need."

"Tell me what it's like to be world champion. Your voice is soothing."

He might have been flattered if Baylor didn't sound half dead. All Chipper was, was scared. Still, he did what he could. "It's humbling. Don't get me wrong, I know I did it. I know how much blood, sweat, and tears went into it, but still. It's humbling. Do you know how few people make it to where I am? Combine that with how badly I wanted it and there're no words." A sad smile pulled at Chipper's lips. "I know I'll lose it one day. That's inevitable. But you have no idea how much I want to hang on to it forever. It's always been my only dream. Where would I even go from here once it's gone?" Chipper had never said any of that to anyone. Any time anyone asked him about upcoming matches, he always tried to play it cool. Truthfully, he was terrified of what was on the other side of the top.

"What do other people do after losing the title?"

Chipper shrugged. "He didn't lose it. He retired, but my friend Maverick trains a few people here and there. Mostly, he just enjoys being with his husband."

"That sounds nice." Baylor slid beneath the water, making Chipper's heart jump into his throat. But he reappeared and slicked back his hair before resting his head on the edge of the tub. "What would you do if you retired?"

This. The thought hit so loud and hard, Chipper stood. He stepped into the closet and found a pair of clean workout shorts. After throwing them on, he returned to Baylor with a few towels and washcloths. He tossed the washcloths in the water and rolled up one towel for Baylor to rest his head.

A sweet smile touched Baylor's features as Chipper tucked the towel beneath his neck. "Thank you. You're avoiding my question."

Chipper shrugged and reclaimed his seat on the floor. "Not really. I just don't know the answer. Maverick seems happy, but I'm not like him. You see me when I have downtime. I'm all over the country, incapable of sitting still."

"You do seem like an unending ball of energy."

Baylor sounded a little better. That kept Chipper talking more than anything. "Nah. I'm actually exhausted, but I don't have anyone to sit still with me. So I visit my friends."

"Sounds lonely."

The observation made Chipper more than a little uncomfortable. "Would you like me to wash your hair?"

Baylor's gorgeous green eyes searched Chipper's face, feeling like the deepest of inspections. "Please? I feel really gross, but I'm also too weak to do anything about it."

Chipper shifted to his knees. "Don't worry. I'm here for you."

Baylor flashed a weak-looking smile. "I know I'm in good hands. That's why I didn't call the cops when you kidnapped me."

An unexpected bark of laughter escaped him. He grabbed the shampoo. "I'd just tell them you were an obsessed fan who jumped in my car like a homeless dog, and I didn't have the heart to drop you."

An adorable snort burst from Baylor. "Fuck. They'd believe you."

Chipper realized he was smiling. Despite everything, he truly enjoyed Baylor's company. Sick or not, Chipper would choose Baylor over anyone. The guy never bored him. It felt like Baylor was exactly where he belonged.

Chapter Four

HE JUST WASN'T GETTING better. Chipper paced the floor, fighting against himself. Baylor could be such a pain in the ass, but he needed a doctor. Chipper wasn't sure he didn't need a hospital. Baylor seemed to get weaker every day. The doorbell rang and Chipper rushed to answer. Nothing happened as quickly as he needed, and his patience was thin. Relief poured through him at the sight of the tall beauty on the other side of the door. His raven black hair had a gloss of money, and his blue eyes were lined with eyeliner. He had two suitcases with him.

Chipper managed a congenial smile. "You must be Sacha." He motioned Sacha inside.

A sharp nod met his statement as he dragged the suitcases across the threshold. "I have Baylor's things. It's really that bad, then?"

The heavy Ukrainian accent might have caught him off guard if they hadn't spoken on the phone several times. Chipper nodded. "He's asleep, which is probably exactly what he needs, but he also needs fluids, and he can't keep anything down. I know he'll be pissed, but I'm about to drag his ass to the doctor."

A wicked-looking smile slowly stretched Sacha's lips. Evil flashed in his eyes. "I like you. He needs a strong hand. Now," Sacha straightened his expensive-looking dress shirt, "as far as business goes, everything is completely under control. I know he's controlling and wants to hover, but I have this until he's better." Sacha held his stare. "Make sure he's actually better before he comes back. I don't want whatever this mess is. I'm an even worse patient than he is." His gaze swept down Chipper's body. "Unless you intend to care for me too." Before Chipper could think of a comeback, Sacha released a dramatic-sounding sigh. "I know. I know. You are feet over tea kettle for Bay. Or however that saying goes. I'll leave you to him."

Chipper shook his head and followed Sacha to the door. He supposed it took a ballsy minx to handle a handful like Baylor. "I'll keep you posted."

"Please do."

After a few more pleasantries, Chipper closed the door, grabbed the suitcases, and headed to face the firing squad. He unpacked the bags first. Chipper wanted to be completely ready for battle. Baylor was too weak to fight, and Chipper wasn't above forcibly dressing him. He would carry him over his shoulder if he had to. Baylor needed help.

With clothes at the ready, he gently shook Baylor. "Hey, gorgeous. Let's get you dressed. Time for the doctor."

Baylor peeked open one eye. "I don't think I can do it." Since Baylor didn't specify what he couldn't do, Chipper assumed he meant everything.

"That's okay. I can do it all, if you're okay with that?"

Baylor's hands rose and fell.

Chipper assumed that was his surrendering gesture. "Don't worry. I won't molest you."

A weak chuckle vibrated from Baylor, making Chipper smile. "That sounds very boring for you."

Chipper couldn't have this conversation while stripping Baylor down to nothing. He'd spent too much time fantasizing over the last year. A thought hit. Maybe Baylor didn't want him because he already had someone. He never considered there might be someone else. Maybe it was Bandit. Dark clouds gathered in his head, darkening his mood. He was worried and frustrated. Chipper wanted to make Baylor better. He wanted Baylor to want him. Fuck. Holding Baylor every night was screwing with his mind. Now he had Baylor nude, dressing him like he would a child. His head was all over the place. He didn't know where he fit. The entire thing was dumb as hell because he was nothing but a nurse in Baylor's eyes.

He didn't even know why he felt so irritated today.

"Why are you angry? It's okay if you don't want to help me."

Chipper fought the demons, trying to swallow him. He managed a small smile. "I'm not mad. You've got me worried."

Baylor didn't respond.

Chipper got him dressed. "There." He met Baylor's beautiful green gaze. Even days of nursing Baylor through a serious illness hadn't dimmed his desire. "In no reality would you bore me. I promise, no matter the circumstances, I'd blow your mind."

Baylor didn't look away. He might have been too weak to bother, but Chipper still savored the moment. By now, Baylor should be more than aware Chipper wanted him. There was no sense in playing coy. Right now wasn't the time, though.

"We need to go."

Baylor nodded.

"Do you need me to carry you?"

"That sounds embarrassing."

Chipper rolled his eyes and scooped him from the bed like he weighed nothing because he did. "How about this? I'll carry you to the car so you can save your strength to walk inside the doctor's office."

"I accept this compromise."

Chipper hummed, fighting a laugh.

Baylor pinched his nipple, probably because it was within reach. "Don't laugh at me."

"I told you, don't abuse me. I'll embarrass you. Don't think I won't stroll into that doctor's office, carrying you just like this, with a huge wet spot on my jeans."

He felt more than heard Baylor's weak laugh. "You're such an idiot."

Maybe, but he was happy again. He locked up the house and got Baylor settled in his truck. It was easier to get Baylor in and out of the larger vehicle. Baylor was silent on the drive. Chipper had a feeling he dozed. The radio played a metal station from his music app. He kept the volume low and worried all the way to the doctor's.

The office was connected to the hospital, making parking a nightmare. He circled the parking garage several times before someone backed from a space. Baylor shook when he stood. Despite his weak protests, he leaned on Chipper. Chipper held more of Baylor's weight than he let on. A guy had his pride. Chipper would let Baylor keep his.

Once they were checked in, they were taken back to a room much faster than Chipper expected. Then again, Baylor looked like hell and they probably didn't want him spreading his germs. They had given him a mask to wear, but still. Baylor really looked awful.

Chipper's knee bobbed in his impatience as they waited for the doctor. A nurse came and drew blood and took what looked to be flu and covid samples. Then they waited and waited some more. Luckily, they had at least given Baylor a blanket and he passed out on the exam table. One of them got to sleep through the wait. Finally, the door swung open after a quick, perfunctory knock. A blond male in his mid-forties stepped inside. His white coat was pristine. He stared at a laptop.

"Mr. Keates?"

Baylor opened his eyes.

The doctor smiled. "I'm Dr. Porter. I hear you've had a bad fever for a few days. What else do you have going on?"

Baylor's eyes flickered Chipper's way.

Chipper took the hint. He was too tired to talk. "He fainted a few times, hasn't been able to keep anything down, and is extremely weak."

Dr. Porter held Chipper's stare and nodded along. When Chipper finished, he grabbed his rolling chair and sat where he could switch his gaze between Baylor and Chipper while he spoke. "Well, both the flu and covid test came back negative." That surprised Chipper. "But obviously, we have something going on. With this high of a fever that doesn't seem to want to break, I'd say it's likely whatever random virus is going around. I can prescribe some anti-viral medication and anti-nausea pills." He clicked around on his laptop. "With that said, some of these numbers on your bloodwork are a bit concerning." He kept his gaze locked on the computer, making it impossible for Chipper to get a read on him. "I'd like to get a bag or two of fluids in you before you leave and then draw some more blood."

"Sounds great." Chipper was beyond relieved at the idea of an IV.

Dr. Porter looked between them again before focusing on Chipper. "So you are..." He left the inquiry hanging. Chipper had no clue what he meant until Baylor responded.

"He's my friend. He's been keeping me alive."

Chipper smirked at getting called a friend. That was a step up from stalker.

The doctor nodded. His gaze swung back Baylor's way. "Good. Part of me is leaning toward admitting you. But if your friend is willing to help, then I'm sure you'd be more comfortable at home. However." He met Chipper's stare, as if trying to emphasize the importance of his words. "If he worsens in any way, take him to the ER. I could likely give him two full bags today and still not pull up these numbers. Getting dehydrated like this can lead to kidney failure and his GFR is in an iffy place."

"What's GFR?" Baylor croaked out.

"It's your kidney function," Chipper answered before the doctor could. His gaze never wavered from the doctor. Chipper's mom had died from kidney disease. "How iffy?"

"Thirty-five."

Well, fuck. "Maybe you should admit him."

"Please don't," Baylor croaked out. "I trust Chipper to take care of me."

The doctor's eyes flickered Baylor's way before focusing on Chipper again. "Why do you look so familiar to me? Are you one of my patients?"

"No."

"He's the MMA light heavyweight world champion." Baylor smirked as he said the words, knowing he had likely doomed Chipper to taking selfies with everyone in the damn building before they got out of there.

Chipper leveled a look at him.

Dr. Porter dismissed the news. "I don't follow sports. It must be something else."

Chipper shot Baylor a triumphant smile before pulling a face and sticking his tongue out at him, childishly enjoying his win. He wouldn't be taking selfies after all. Still, he chose to put the doctor out of his misery.

"We met at The Aviator." Truthfully, Chipper had thought the doctor had known him by his title that night. It seemed the guy had simply wanted to fuck him.

The doctor stiffened. His gaze moved from the laptop where he had been happily tapping along, oblivious to Baylor and Chipper's childishness. He eyed Chipper. "I don't recall."

Chipper nearly laughed. *Liar*.

He snapped his laptop closed and stood. "I'll get these orders put in." His gaze stayed locked on Baylor, pretending Chipper didn't exist now that his memory had obviously cleared. "Remember what I said. If you get worse, what do you do?"

"Go to the ER," Baylor repeated back dutifully.

With a sharp nod and completely ignoring Chipper, he left them alone. Chipper probably should have kept his mouth shut. He really wanted the guy to make Baylor better. Thankfully, he seemed like a professional, despite trying to take Chipper home five minutes after his wife left the club.

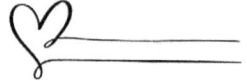

Baylor ground his back teeth. He didn't want to be irritated on top of being sick, but goddamn it. For a moment, he had felt a flicker of something growing between them. Even obviously on his deathbed, Chipper made him hot. More than that, he had fucked with Baylor's heart by holding him all night, every night. Dr. Porter was a stark reminder of why Baylor had avoided Chipper.

"Maybe I should just let them admit me and get out of your hair."

Chipper's gaze moved over his face, studying him. "You're angry with me."

Before Baylor could lie and deny, the door opened, and a nurse came in, rolling an IV pole. Baylor ground his back teeth while she hooked him up and started the drip.

"This'll take about forty-five minutes to empty, and Dr. Porter ordered two. So, settle in." She focused on Chipper, because everyone did. "If you head to the second floor, you can follow the signs to the hospital cafeteria if you need anything."

Chipper nodded his thanks. "I appreciate the info."

She flashed a flirtatious smile before heading out.

Baylor rolled his eyes.

Chipper didn't let their conversation go. The moment the door closed, he was both feet in. "Why are you mad at me?"

Baylor counted to five. He would not sound like a jealous teenager. Baylor was a grown man, and he didn't even want to be with Chipper. "The doctor? Really?" Fuck it. He felt too bad to hold back. "Have you slept with everyone?"

The way Chipper's expression closed—so quickly and coldly—made Baylor realize immediately he had been wrong. When Chipper spoke, he sounded different, as if talking to a stranger. Baylor hated it. "No. I haven't slept with everyone, and I didn't sleep with your doctor. He's acting cagey because he tried to get me to go home with him five minutes after his wife left the club. I know it's hard to believe, but I'm not—" Chipper stopped dead, as if he suddenly realized it wasn't worth it. He looked away and stood. "Do you want anything from the cafeteria?"

"Please don't."

Chipper nodded while still not looking at him. "You're right. I doubt you could keep it down." He took a step toward the door.

"That's not what I meant," Baylor blurted out. He couldn't watch Chipper walk away. Baylor was sick and weepy and scared about whatever they said about his kidneys. He felt out of the loop and guilty for hurting Chipper. "I'm sorry. When it comes to work, I'm a genius. Otherwise, I'm pretty bad at life. I didn't mean to hurt you. That's not something I'd ever want to do." He swallowed. "It's okay if you need to walk away from me for a minute, but please don't leave. I'm scared, and you're the only thing holding me together."

Chipper never once looked his way through his speech. That made it easier for Baylor to be honest. He wasn't good at being vulnerable. If he wasn't sick and his defenses weren't down, he would never.

Chipper changed directions and grabbed the rolling stool. He sat and rolled to Baylor's side. Baylor was on his side on the hard-ass table, curled into a ball. Chipper took his hand and set his chin on the edge of the table. He held Baylor's stare, looking like the giant puppy he was.

"I've given you plenty of reasons to think the worst of me."

Baylor shook his head. "You've given me more to think the best. I don't trust people easily."

Chipper snorted. Even that was hot. "You don't say?"

Baylor laughed. "Oh, God. Don't make me laugh. Everything hurts."

Chipper rubbed his arm. "These fluids should make you feel better. Most of your weakness is probably dehydration."

"I wish that doctor had explained the kidney stuff before running away."

Chipper winced. "Sorry. I have a hard time letting cheats act like they're not, but I shouldn't have said anything. Looks like, right now, you have thirty-five percent kidney function. As he said, severe dehydration will shut down your kidneys. So, these fluids should bring your numbers back up. Don't worry."

Baylor nodded. He didn't know why he found Chipper so comforting, but if he said everything was okay, then it would be. "I hope I don't end up giving this to you. This has been awful."

A gorgeous smile stretched Chipper's lips. "Will you take care of me if you do?"

"I can't carry you around."

"And you don't want to miss more work," Chipper tacked on.

Baylor wouldn't confirm that. He knew he was a bad person, but he probably wouldn't miss work. "Have I kept you from anything?"

Chipper shrugged. "I got a fight coming up, but I can train at home."

"How do you usually train?" While Baylor mostly asked questions so he could have something else to focus on, he genuinely wanted to know. He wanted to know everything about Chipper.

"My buddy, Maverick, he's won heavyweight champion too many times for me to count. He helps me. We spar and whatnot."

"I should let you get back to that, and get some work done too. Our careers shouldn't suffer because of a virus."

Chipper's gaze moved over Baylor's face. He didn't fuss the way he normally did when Baylor mentioned getting back to work. When he spoke, he sounded curious. "If you were getting married, who would you want to plan your wedding?"

"Me."

Chipper rolled his eyes. "I mean, if you were forced to hire someone else, who would you hire?"

"Sacha," Baylor answered without thinking about it. He had trained Sacha, and he was the best.

Chipper nodded. "Then why in the hell are you acting like Sacha can't handle things while you heal?"

The question made him look too hard at himself, and Baylor never liked what he saw when he did that. "Maybe I'm a control freak." The way Chipper stared at him—like he saw Baylor to his core broke him. "Or maybe, if I stop, all I have is me and who wants to be around that guy?" He chuckled, making light of his true feelings. Baylor couldn't help it. All the therapy in the world couldn't fix some things. It couldn't change the past.

"Me."

Baylor's breath caught at the surety in Chipper's voice. He meant it. Before he could think of a way to respond, the door opened. The nurse returned to change out the bag. Baylor hadn't realized how long they had been talking. There was one thing he had realized, though. He didn't want to lose Chipper when he got well. No one other than Bandit saw him the way Chipper did. He didn't want that to go away.

Chapter Five

HEALING WAS TAKING SO long. Baylor had convinced himself he would never get better. But he also became a little more aware every day of the body that held him each night. Cuddling became less about warmth and more about need. Maybe Baylor hadn't eaten much in a week and a half, but Chipper had forced water in him, and these goddamn tattooed abs were making him insane. They were too close for Baylor's sanity.

He knew Chipper wasn't asleep. There was a stillness in the air that didn't exist when

Chipper slept. It was like the entire universe held its breath, waiting to see what Chipper did next. He was such a goofy force of nature. Surely, he fascinated the universe every bit as much as he did Baylor. With zero permission from his brain, Baylor's fingertips skimmed the abs he wanted to lick. Chipper's muscles tensed for a second, as if surprised by the touch.

Embarrassment had Baylor making up excuses. "How many years has it taken to get all these tattoos?"

Chipper sounded groggy when he responded, as if he had almost been asleep. It was no wonder he flinched at Baylor's touch. Baylor felt guilty. "I started as soon as I turned eighteen, so fourteen years."

So he was thirty-two. Baylor felt like he should have known that. He forced his eyes closed. Chipper needed sleep. Baylor was the only one who had slept nonstop for over a week. His mind didn't want to stop zooming. That wasn't Chipper's problem.

"I've tried so hard to be respectful when I help you dress. I've never noticed. Do you have any ink?"

Chipper always left the bathroom light on and the door slightly ajar. It lit the room enough for them to see at night without tripping on the way to the bathroom. Baylor took off his shirt and rolled so Chipper could see his back. His eyes fell closed and chill bumps rose on his skin when Chipper traced the numbers above the soccer ball on his back.

"What's this date?"

A tear slipped from the corner of his eye and landed on the bed. Baylor hadn't thought he had any left to shed. "I lost a bet." He cleared his throat. "I think I should get out of your hair tomorrow. You still have some time left before your fight to train. You'll get more done without me here."

Warm lips touched his shoulder.

A shaky breath fell from Baylor's lips. Baylor could only end up hurting Chipper, but he didn't know how to say no. It had been so long since anyone touched him. He had nothing to offer, but Chipper's mouth felt perfect on his skin. At some point, Chipper had slipped beneath his walls. He didn't have the strength to shove him out again.

Chipper scooted closer. His hard body molded against Baylor's back. A warm breath caressed his ear as Chipper kissed its shell. Baylor felt like he would fly apart into a thousand pieces any second.

"Tell me what you need to stay."

Something shattered inside Baylor. He heard the pieces fall inside his head like a broken mirror slipping from its frame. What did it matter? There was nothing left of him to take.

Baylor rolled. His mouth found Chipper's. Chipper's hands stayed polite. His kiss was disrespectful as hell. If Baylor had any strength to stop before that moment, it vanished with a swipe of Chipper's tongue. With the slightest push, Baylor was beneath him. There was nothing between them except their thin pajama pants. A random thought hit from nowhere. He had been well enough to sleep in another room for a few days now. Chipper didn't have to hold him to keep him warm or watch him to keep him alive. Baylor chose Chipper's bed. It was a huge betrayal.

Baylor pushed at Chipper's chest. Panic threatened to choke the life from him.

Chipper immediately rolled away, giving him space. "Are you okay? I shouldn't have pawed at you while you're still sick. I'm so sorry."

Baylor sucked air, fighting the anxiety attack. It wasn't Chipper's fault. He couldn't let such a great guy think he had done anything wrong. "You're fine. Sorry." He took a few more breaths. His teeth started to chatter. He hadn't gotten this bad in months. "Sorry," he said again.

"Stop apologizing and tell me what's wrong." He rubbed Baylor's arms. He looked so worried. Baylor didn't know how to say any of the words he needed to say.

"I just need a minute." He rolled from the bed and headed for the bathroom. In the safety of the locked bathroom, Baylor gripped the edge of the sink. He couldn't look at his reflection. If he caught sight of the pain in his eyes, it would be real. He couldn't survive it being real. His panicked gaze shot around the room. He had to get out. Baylor had to get away before he destroyed an amazing man. Chipper didn't deserve this.

His gaze landed on the door that led to the next bedroom. He didn't hesitate. Baylor had to be fast. Baylor turned the water on in the sink to cover the sound of his leaving and darted for the door. All the years of sneaking out of the house as a teen came to his rescue now. Once he was down the hall, he was home free. His phone was on the kitchen counter and his shoes were by the door. Baylor didn't need anything else. Everything else was replaceable. He shot out the back door and was down the street before he took a full breath. Too late, he realized he had left his wallet behind. Baylor sat on the curb and covered his eyes. The tears came. Sobs racked his body. He didn't even understand himself. How could he explain anything to Chipper? There were some truths that could never be repeated.

Just as he somehow knew he would, Chipper appeared from nowhere. He looked stoic and way too fucking understanding. With the smallest effort, he scooped Baylor from the ground and headed back inside. He didn't question Baylor or lecture him. Chipper simply took off Baylor's shoes and put him back to bed. When he walked away, Baylor fought the urge to beg him not to go. But Chipper was back in no time, the way he always was. He brought a warm washcloth and cleaned Baylor's face. Afterward, he climbed back into bed and went back to holding Baylor.

He kissed Baylor's temple. "Close your eyes. I'll get you home to Bandit tomorrow."

For a long while, Baylor stared at the ceiling. As always, the anger and bitterness set in. Life was so goddamn unfair. Chipper deserved better than the broken man he held.

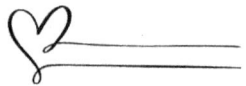

There wasn't a chance in hell Chipper would sleep after that. He had no clue what happened, but he would find out. When Chipper had a goal, he was like a dog with a bone. He didn't give up and the mystery of Baylor had him in its grip. Part of him wondered if Baylor was in love with Bandit. They were best friends, but they didn't seem inseparable or anything. Bandit wasn't here taking care of Baylor. But Chipper had a bad feeling, whatever was happening, Baylor needed Bandit more than him. He had a soccer ball tattooed on his back, for fuck's sake. Chipper couldn't compete with whatever they had.

"I'd like to try again."

The quietly spoken words shocked the hell out of Chipper. His determination had Chipper's brain completely switching gears. Had someone hurt Baylor? It was one explanation that fit his behavior. If so, he put a hell of a lot of trust in Chipper. Chipper had a lot of self-control. He could pull out all the stops to make Baylor comfortable.

"If that's what you want." Chipper made no move to touch him. "You're in charge, though. That way, you can stop anywhere you like. Don't worry about me. I can take a lot of abuse."

A weak chuckle burst from Baylor like a huff. "Abuse? I suppose that's fair." He rolled Chipper's way. His fingers skimmed

Chipper's stomach. "From the first time we met, I guess I've been a little difficult."

"Apparently, I like my men a little mean."

Baylor pinched him.

Chipper rubbed the spot like it hurt, even though it didn't. "See? Abuse."

"You're right." He kissed the place he pinched. His lips lingered. Chipper hoped like hell he hadn't been lying to himself about that control. He wanted Baylor more than he had ever wanted anyone.

"I take it back. You're passionate."

He felt Baylor smile against his skin. "That's better." His mouth moved to Chipper's collarbone. "You're beautiful. I know you know that, but it's from the inside out."

Chipper smiled. "I don't know how to feel. You complimented me and called me conceited at the same time."

"Not conceited." He licked Chipper's neck, making him pant. "Confident. Don't worry. Confidence is sexy. Your eyes are amazing. They're almost at odds with the rest of you. They're soft and sweet with the most gorgeous lashes. But the eyes are the window to the soul, or so they say. With you, it's true."

Fuck. He got the feeling Baylor needed to keep talking to stay grounded, but Chipper never expected Baylor to make him feel like this. Like he was special. "You have beautiful eyes too. That's the first thing I noticed about you. Your gorgeous eyes flashed with fire and so much annoyance when we met."

He felt more than heard Baylor chuckle against his skin. Baylor's hand slipped inside Chipper's pants unexpectedly. Chipper prayed for strength. Baylor lightly stroked him before pushing Chipper's pants down. Chipper lifted just enough to make Baylor's job easier. His skin was on fire. He still didn't know if this would go anywhere. Chipper feared for his sanity.

Baylor sucked his neck. "If I start crying again, please don't think it has anything to do with you. I'm trying really hard to find my way, but I don't want to stop."

Yeah. He was going to die. Chipper had never been so aware of anyone's touch. "If you need to stop, I'll be okay." Chipper was pretty sure that was the biggest lie he had ever told.

"I know you want me to be in charge, but I don't know where anything is—like condoms or whatever."

Damn. Chipper would have to get involved, and he worried Baylor would stop touching him again the moment he became the aggressor in any way. "Tell me what you want. Step by step, so I don't go too far."

Baylor pulled back and cocked his head. He studied Chipper's face for a moment. "I'm not scared of you." A sad smile touched his lips. "I'm just fucked up. You deserve more than I might be able to give. Please don't think any of my bullshit is on you. It isn't. You're amazing and I want you. I'm just..." For a moment, Baylor looked beyond lost and broken. "I want you," he repeated. "You should get that condom."

Chipper didn't need to be told again. He rolled and pulled open the bedside drawer. Once he had the lube and a condom, he rolled back, half expecting his thirty-second distraction had changed the mood again. Instead, he found Baylor nude.

His gaze slid down Baylor's body, taking in the gorgeous skin and dark hair. "Goddamn. You're stunning."

Baylor skimmed his fingertips down Chipper's arm. His gaze followed the path of his fingers. A quick smile passed over his lips. "If you don't get sick after this, you're fucking immortal."

A laugh burst from Chipper. It quickly died as he realized Baylor probably felt too bad to be doing this. "Are you sure you're up for this?"

Baylor stroked his erection, making Chipper's mouth water. "I'm definitely up, but you'll have to do the work. My energy is zapped. I probably shouldn't have gone for an impromptu run." A wry smile touched his lips. "I have no idea why you want me. You must be completely insane."

Chipper shifted positions, going up on his knees. He kissed Baylor's stomach. "I get my ass kicked for a living. Are you just now figuring out I'm crazy? Life on the edge, baby. That's the only life for me." He licked Baylor's cock, lingering for a moment to worship his crown. The shaky way Baylor breathed was like music to his ears. He blindly opened the condom and rolled it down his length. Chipper had to keep Baylor distracted and interested. He flipped open the tube of lube and coated the condom. Chipper planned each move the same way he did on the mat. Baylor had panicked when Chipper had been on top of him. This time, he hooked Baylor's knee and used his training against him. He quickly twisted Baylor's body while he slipped his hips beneath him. In a matter of seconds, he had Baylor on his side and his cock seeking entrance.

Baylor reached over his shoulder and cupped the back of Chipper's head, pulling him closer and silently begging for more.

Chipper kissed his neck as he slowly pushed his way inside. Baylor was so fucking tight, and Chipper hadn't taken the time he should to get him ready. In his heart, he knew if he had tried, Baylor would have freaked out again. Baylor wasn't panicking now. He pushed back, trying to take what he wanted. Chipper couldn't breathe. Baylor felt incredible.

"You're so much better than I imagined."

Baylor chuckled. It was a winded sound, reminding Chipper that Baylor wasn't at a hundred percent. Hell, he probably wasn't at thirty. "How often have you imagined?"

Chipper thrust, going root deep. A growl escaped him as possessiveness overtook him. "Every goddamn day since the moment I first saw you."

Baylor shook.

Chipper pumped inside him with shallow thrusts, trying not to abuse him. He was small and felt delicate. Chipper had never been more aware of his strength. Baylor felt fragile in his arms. Precious. Chipper needed to savor the moment. Worship his obsession. He couldn't stop kissing every place he could reach.

Baylor tried pushing back again, restless in his arms. "Please?"

"Say what you want. You have to be in charge." If Baylor wanted to stop now because Chipper went too far, Chipper would perish. No dramatics. He was a man on the edge.

"Fuck me. I won't break."

That was all the permission Chipper needed. He rolled, forcing Baylor to his knees. He dug his knees into the bed for traction and slammed inside Baylor. The satisfied moan that sounded like it came from Baylor's soul told him everything. Baylor liked it rough. Chipper obliged. He held Baylor's hips and pounded his ass. Hip control was a big factor in martial arts. He knew how to hold the perfect position and angle for as long as Baylor needed. The sounds coming from Baylor got more desperate by the second. Chipper ground his back teeth to a pulp. He was inside Baylor—the man he had craved and stalked—and his body knew it.

Baylor scratched at the sheets. His cries turned muffled, as if he bit the bed. Chipper couldn't take it. He was too close and every move Baylor made was too sexy. He reached around and grabbed Baylor's cock. Chipper stroked, beating his dick like he jacked himself off. Baylor's body suddenly clenched so tightly, Chipper saw stars and then a cry bounced from the walls. Baylor's asshole tried sucking him deeper. A loud groan tore from his throat as cum shot from him with a force that nearly blinded him. As they collapsed into a gasping heap,

Chipper turned at the last second, ensuring his weight didn't land on Baylor.

With his arm and leg thrown across Baylor's sweat-covered body, he fought to catch his breath. It was odd. He could go rounds on the mat without getting winded. This was something else. Baylor had stolen the air from his lungs and the soul from his body.

He ran his fingers through Baylor's hair. Baylor was too quiet. "Are you okay?"

"I don't think I can move."

Panic hit Chipper. Had he been too rough? He jumped to his knees and rolled Baylor to his back. Baylor genuinely seemed to be made of rubber. He was like a lifeless doll. "I'm sorry. You should've told me to stop. I would never hurt you. Tell me what to do."

Baylor laughed. It came out as a wheeze. "I'm fine. I'm just covered in cum and now I'm just chilling in the wet spot without a single working muscle. This virus will be the death of me."

Chipper's shoulders sagged. He had honestly thought he had done some sort of damage. Chipper shook his head and stole a kiss. "I'd never let you die." He kissed Baylor's chin. "I'd also never make you sleep in the wet spot. Don't worry. I can get you cleaned up, and these sheets changed without you having to move a muscle. You'd be surprised at how adept I am."

Baylor's arm lifted. His hand shook as he ran his fingers through Chipper's hair. "No. I wouldn't. Nothing you do could surprise me. I'm fully convinced you're magic."

Chipper's throat swelled. There was something in Baylor's eyes. Like he had said, they were the window to the soul. Chipper got his first good look at Baylor's. It was totally shattered.

Chapter Six

CHIPPER: *I MISS YOU **already.***

Chipper: *Call me.*

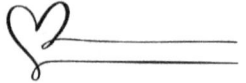

Chipper: *I thought it would take longer for you to start dodging me again.*

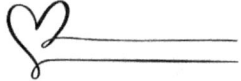

Chipper: *I really need you to answer my calls. It's important.*

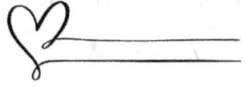

Chipper: *I'm in town. You around to talk?*

Bandit: *Yeah. I'm at Jamestown Field, practicing with a few teammates. Swing by. We'll be here a while.*

Chipper: *Thanks, man. I'll be there in ten.*

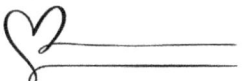

There had been a hint of worry in the back of Chipper's mind that Baylor would go right back to his old ways the moment he was out of sight. He had really hoped their one night together would change that. Even though he had known Baylor wasn't well yet, he hadn't argued when Baylor said he needed to leave the next morning. It was obvious Baylor needed space to clear his head, and he couldn't avoid work forever. There had always been a time when Baylor would leave. Chipper had to be realistic on that one. But damn, this totally ignoring him shit drove him up the wall, especially when he had a valid reason to try to reach him. Bandit was his only hope of finding him. If Baylor wouldn't answer his calls, he would damn well see him. He knew if he sat down with Bandit, Bandit would help him with the situation.

The field where Bandit practiced was a pro field. It was regulation everything, set up to host games of any level. Bandit had said a few teammates, but it looked like the whole team to him. A stack of gym bags filled with gear littered a certain section of seats on the sidelines. That was where Chipper chose to sit and wait. He watched Bandit pass the ball from foot to foot before doing some sort of trick kick toward the net. Without looking to see if he made it, Bandit turned his way and jogged to the sidelines.

He was all smiles as he grabbed the seat next to him. "Hey." Bandit didn't sound winded in the least.

Chipper was impressed. "Hey. You look great out there."

Bandit's huge grin reminded Chipper of a kid. The guy was tall and skinny with red hair and freckles, but he had somehow ended up with blue eyes. If Baylor was in love with him, Chipper guessed he could see why. He wasn't bad looking on top of having been by Baylor's side for years. Chipper liked him. If Baylor chose him, Chipper wasn't sure he could hate him.

"Don't you have a fight coming up?"

"In three weeks."

Bandit stared at the guys on the field as if he looked for weaknesses.

Chipper couldn't take it anymore. He had to know if this was who made Baylor cry with longing. "What's the date on Baylor's back?"

Bandit glanced his way. "His son's birthday." He dropped the words so easily—like it should be common knowledge.

"His son?" Chipper sounded as surprised as he was, and he didn't have time to stop it. A son? That was... not at all what he expected.

For a moment, Bandit simply stared at him with a blank expression. Finally, he blew out a sigh and looked away. "That tracks. I don't suppose Bay has talked to anyone at all about anything other than weddings since Micah died."

The knot that had begun to tighten in his stomach at hearing Baylor had a son completely gripped him now, leaving him helpless in the face of that bomb.

Thankfully, Bandit didn't need Chipper's encouragement to keep talking. "See, the first thing you have to understand about Bay is he has never had anyone, except me, but I'm just me." Chipper had no idea what that meant and Bandit didn't explain. He just kept going.

"Bay was raised by foster parents who were even more abusive than the parents he'd been taken from. The minute he was free to leave, he came to live with my family, but he never had anyone love him who should have. I got picked up by New England and we stuck together. I've always tried to be as close to family as I can be. He's my best friend. I love him. There's nothing I wouldn't do for him. So, when he started working on his event planning business, I was like his one-man hype team. I knew, still know, he can do anything he sets his mind to. He's pretty amazing." He looked Chipper's way just long enough to get Chipper's nod of agreement before going back to watching his team. Thankfully, he kept talking. Chipper needed to know everything.

"Anyhow, a player on my team was talking to me about wanting to throw a huge party for his son's first birthday. So I told Freddie about Bay, singing his praises. Then I introduced them." Bandit stared at nothing and shook his head. A small smile played on his lips.

"I've never seen anything like it. They had such an instant connection. Real love at first sight. Freddie had Micah through a surrogate while in a long-term relationship, only to get abandoned before he was born.

Bay took one look at Freddie and Micah, and they took one look at him. Boom. They were beautiful. They were married so fast, it nearly spun my head, and Baylor immediately adopted Micah. Freddie was the home and love Baylor always deserved."

Chipper didn't know why it took Bandit saying Freddie's name so many times for it to hit him. Chipper knew everyone. He went to every celebrity wedding trying to get closer to Baylor. But he got invited to those events for a reason. He knew everyone. He had met Freddie Keates years ago, before he had his son. A pain sliced through his chest. Freddie and his three-year-old son were killed in a car accident a few years back. The loss of a famous soccer player and his baby was big news at the time.

"I remember Freddie. He came to one of my matches years ago and introduced himself afterward."

Bandit turned his head and met Chipper's stare. There was something dark in Bandit's eyes. "He was on his way to Bay. That night, when they died," he clarified unnecessarily. "Bay's business had more than taken off by then, and Freddie traveled for games. It was hard, but they actively worked at it every day. I've never seen a stronger marriage. Freddie and Bay were supposed to meet halfway that night so they could have one night together as a family. Then Micah was supposed to stay with Bay so Freddie could head to Colorado for a game." Bandit looked away again. "As you know, they never made it, and you see what's left of Bay. He shoved everything in storage except for the barest necessities and lost himself in work." He shook his head. "For the past three years, I've told myself this was better than the alternative. He would be dead without that outlet." Bandit's gaze swung Chipper's way again, and it hit Chipper. He knew he recognized the pain in Bandit's eyes. It was what he saw every time he looked at Baylor. Bandit held his stare. "The thing is, he might be alive, but he doesn't want it. He'll work until he drops dead, then be thankful for it. If you hadn't saved him when you did, and nursed him back to health, he would've accepted that fate. He has nothing. That business means nothing. I mean nothing. This whole world could fuck off. He died alongside the only people who ever loved him exactly the way he needs. If you saw that tattoo, then you've been closer to him than anyone has since they passed. If you don't save him, no one can, and just like me, you'll have to accept he's not long for this world. I've been waiting on that call for a long time."

Chipper looked away and focused on the field. "I'm trying, but he keeps running. I don't even know where he is."

Bandit stood and grabbed a nearby bag of gear. He dug through it and came out with a set of keys. "He's at my place. Good luck."

Hope surged through Chipper as his fingers wrapped around the keys. He knew what he was up against now and Chipper didn't know how to quit. "I've got this."

Bandit smiled. "I know."

The person closest to Baylor believed. Chipper couldn't lose.

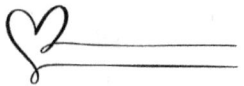

Depression lived heavily on Baylor's chest all hours of the day. While that was a familiar state, this was different. Work wasn't saving him anymore. Chipper had kicked the door open, reminding him how love felt, and he couldn't shut it out. Feelings bombarded him. He listened to Chipper's voicemails over and over, hearing the desperation in his voice and guilt ate at him. Baylor didn't know if it was for betraying Freddie or ignoring Chipper. It was ridiculous how bad he still felt after his illness, and that added another layer to his inability to think straight. He had honestly believed coming to stay with Bandit would help. It always had in the past. Nothing soothed him now. Nothing distracted him. It was just Baylor and reality, and the reality was, he had feelings for Chipper.

He heard Bandit's keys turn in the door. Baylor tried to hide his emotions. Bandit had dealt with his issues their entire lives. He had to be so exhausted by Baylor.

The door swung open, and Chipper stepped inside. Baylor's heart stopped and then soared. The way he felt at the sight of Chipper said so much more than all the overthinking in the world. He couldn't hide from this.

Chipper's gaze landed on Baylor. His hard expression was new and didn't give Baylor hope. It looked like he was done with Baylor's bullshit and that was completely fair. Baylor was tired too. Chipper didn't bother saying hello.

"You don't know how to answer a damn phone?" He sliced his hand through the air, silencing Baylor before he even had time to respond. "Obviously, you forgot you have an appointment to check your kidney function tomorrow. FYI, my mom died when her kidneys shut down because she was too stubborn to accept she was sick, and you're not doing that shit to me too. So, stand up, get your shit, and get in the damn car so we can fly back home. You have exactly five minutes, or so help me, I will carry your ass out of here. Do you understand?"

He hadn't known about Chipper's mom. Now he had a new guilt to add to the list. "You're right. I forgot."

"Four and half minutes."

Damn. He really was mad. A tiny part of Baylor wanted to call his bluff, except Baylor knew Chipper didn't play like that. Baylor stood. Luckily, he was still mostly packed. It didn't take much to gather his things. Chipper followed on his heels, blatantly supervising, as if scared Baylor might sneak out a window. He deserved that.

Chipper picked up his prescription bottles and checked them. "At least you've taken your meds."

It was easy to remember two more pills when he already took all the crazy drugs. He imagined that was his biggest problem right now. Baylor hadn't taken his meds while he stayed with Chipper. He had been so sick; it hadn't even occurred to him until his mental health took a dive. Now he had to get the happy pills pumping through his system again before he stepped into traffic.

Chipper helped gather his things.

Baylor didn't argue. The truth was, he belonged with Chipper. He knew that now because it felt like he packed to go home. Things were a little more tense than he liked, though. Chipper didn't really speak, and that wasn't like him.

Bandit came through the door as Chipper dragged his bags outside. He watched Chipper go before focusing on Baylor. "Good. You've come to your senses."

Baylor smiled despite himself. Bandit never pulled any punches. "I forgot I have a doctor's appointment in California tomorrow, but I'll see you again soon. You know I can't stay away."

Bandit hugged him and kissed the top of his head. "I know. That's who we are. We're twin flames or whatever the fuck that street psychic yelled at us that one time."

Baylor laughed against Bandit's chest, but it was true. Sometimes a person's other half was a friend. Bandit was irreplaceable. He gave Bandit a final squeeze. "I love you."

"I love you too, babe. Now go before Chipper throws you over his shoulder."

With a laugh, Baylor headed for the door. He knew Chipper would do exactly that if he didn't move his ass. Chipper stood next to an unfamiliar SUV, holding open the passenger door. Baylor assumed it was a rental. He climbed inside and put on his seatbelt like a good boy.

Chipper didn't speak to him again until they were halfway to the airport and Baylor couldn't leap from the car. "Why did you lie to me about the date on your back?"

He supposed this conversation had always been inevitable. "I didn't lie. I bet every ounce of myself on love and lost."

"I knew Freddie. He seemed like a great guy."

Baylor smiled. Of course, Chipper knew Freddie. Chipper never sat still and knew everyone. Baylor realized he was smiling. Chipper had said Freddie's name and all he felt was grateful two of the best men he had ever known knew each other. Chipper was exactly the kind of guy Freddie would have adored. They were a lot alike.

"He was a huge goofball. I'd never had anyone in my life like him before we met. It was a refreshing change from getting my ass

116

kicked every day. I don't think anyone can understand that unless they've been there."

"You're allowed to say things like that to me."

Baylor chuckled. There was no humor in the sound. "I don't think you listened when I told you not to take my mental instability personally." He motioned toward his head even though Chipper watched the road. "This is a mess. I've done all the therapy and taken all the meds. Some things are unfixable. I want to talk about them, but the words choke me." He ran his hand down Chipper's arm and linked fingers with him. Chipper cast him a quick glance and Baylor didn't let go. "If I could talk to anyone, it would be you. You make me feel things and that's terrifying. When you kissed me that first time, I felt like I betrayed them. You're the only person I've let touch me since they died." Baylor dropped his gaze to his lap, but he didn't release Chipper's hand. It seemed he had more to say than he realized. He had to stop before he cried again. The tears were so bottomless. He was so exhausted.

Chipper kissed his hand.

Baylor smiled to himself. He closed his eyes and savored Chipper's lips on his skin. Freddie would have wanted this for him. He would never want Baylor to cry like this and spend his life alone. In fact, he felt like Freddie had handpicked Chipper. Chipper was the kind of guy Freddie respected. It was Baylor who couldn't let go.

"I don't know why I haven't been able to stay away from you. This is the first time I've made a complete ass of myself to be close to someone. The party you're throwing for Eric started as only a way to see you. On my end, of course. Obviously, Oakley wants to throw a huge party for Eric, but I just wanted to see you. Tell me why you haven't let anyone else touch you since Freddie, and

I've never felt like this about anyone. Is that only a coincidence?"

Chipper was this huge child who kicked people's ass for a living, but he was also a goddamn adult. He communicated. It was a good thing he was strong because Baylor was weak as hell. Chipper's solid personality made him braver. "No. I don't think it's a coincidence."

Chipper kissed Baylor's hand again. "Okay. I'll keep fighting for this, then, as long as you'll fight a little for me too."

Baylor tugged Chipper's arm to his side of the car and hugged it. He kissed his bicep. "I'm sorry I panicked and didn't answer your texts or calls."

Chipper looked his way and winked. "Don't worry. I have a reason to spank you now."

Baylor laughed, but he felt way more than simple humor. He wished he could vocalize the growing emotions crushing him. Chipper deserved to hear how he felt. He had to start somewhere. "This feels a hell of a lot like fate, so yeah. Whatever is left of me will fight for that."

Chipper gave a sharp nod. "Okay. We have a plan, sort of."

A laugh burst from Baylor. They were such a mess. He didn't think either of them knew what the hell they were doing. They would do it, nonetheless. What they had was too rare, at least on Baylor's end. He just had to be a little brave. Baylor knew Chipper would take care of the rest.

Chapter Seven

As THEY CAME THROUGH the door, Chipper watched Baylor's shoulders relax—like coming home. He recognized how much Baylor needed someone to simply take over his life. Otherwise, he would go right back to working himself to death. Chipper dragged Baylor's suitcases straight to the bedroom and set to unpacking them. Baylor sat on the bed and watched as Chipper found drawers for him and hung clothes in the closet.

"Is this everything you own, or should I hire a moving company?"

Baylor twisted his fingers, but he didn't argue. "I keep clothes at Bandit's place, but they stay there for a reason. It's easier when I'm working in that area. Otherwise, everything I own is in storage." Baylor visibly swallowed. "I haven't opened that storage unit in three years and I'm not sure I'll ever find the strength to..." Baylor swallowed again and looked away. "I can't look at Micah's things. His toys." Baylor blew out a breath. He swiped at his eyes and met Chipper's gaze. He chuckled. "Why do you want this?"

Even though Chipper knew he was just trying to lighten the mood with the question, he sat next to him and did his best to answer. "You know how I talked to you about losing my title? I've never told anyone that." He looked Baylor's way and held his stare. "You're under my skin in a way no one else has ever been." He shrugged. "If you need me to tell you that every day, I will."

Baylor leaned his way and leaned his head on Chipper's shoulder. "Thank you."

"For what?" Chipper was legit confused by his gratitude. His motives were purely selfish. He couldn't let Baylor go.

"For being uniquely you. I wish I had known we would end up here. There's no way I can get tickets to watch your match on this short of notice. I checked," he added with a laugh.

"Actually, you couldn't get tickets two minutes after they went on sale. Lucky for you, though, I can bring guests."

Baylor's sexy eyes focused on him. "Yay." The soft cheer didn't even penetrate Chipper's brain. Baylor shifted positions. He moved to his knees and straddled Chipper's lap. Chipper immediately grabbed Baylor's ass to hold him in place. Baylor wrapped his arms around Chipper's neck. Chipper's heart sped. His breathing shallowed. Baylor bumped noses with him before kissing the corner of his mouth. Chipper waited with bated breath. It was worth it. Baylor's tongue swept over his bottom lip before he nibbled. Chipper's lips parted. Baylor slipped inside. That was when Chipper took control.

Trusting in their newfound strength after their talk, Chipper rolled. With Baylor beneath him, he took the kiss he wanted. He licked the roof of Baylor's mouth, teasing him. His cock knocked at the zipper of his jeans, begging to be set free. Chipper ignored it while memorizing every move Baylor's tongue made.

His phone buzzed. It took Chipper a second to feel it with the way Baylor had his body tingling. With a growl, Chipper sat back on his knees and dug out the device. He planned to turn it off and toss it aside until he saw the name on the face.

"Oh shit. Oh no."

"What?" Baylor sounded breathless, and he still touched Chipper everywhere he could, but he looked concerned.

"I forgot I have a training session with Maverick today."

Baylor motioned him away. "Go. This is important."

His gaze locked on Baylor. He wasn't ready to let him out of his sight yet. An idea struck. "Come with me." His hopes immediately died. "It'll probably be boring, though."

"No. I'm not worried about that. Let's go. Just text Maverick and let him know we're running late. You can blame me, if you want. Tell him I've been sick, and you're scared to let me out of your sight. I held you up by moving slower than usual."

Chipper shook his head, but he couldn't stop smiling. Baylor was a dream come true. "Thankfully, he doesn't live far." He climbed from the bed and helped Baylor to his feet. Baylor looked beautifully mussed. Chipper fought the urge to blow off Maverick. Baylor had him headed to the door before he could change his mind. They would be great together.

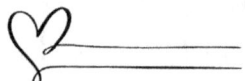

As much as Baylor wanted to jump Chipper and beg him to turn around so they could pick up where they left off, Chipper had made that career admission to him.

Baylor couldn't unlearn that. He cared about Chipper. That meant Chipper's match mattered to him. He looked forward to seeing Chipper in action.

As Maverick's house came into view, Baylor sat forward. He had worked with countless wealthy clients, but this was next level. The place was an estate. A compound. It was massive and beautiful. The place overlooked the water and had security out the ass.

"Um, is this champion money?"

Chipper's laughing gaze swung his way. "I wish. No. Maverick's husband owns hotel casinos all over the country. He's the owner of Luna."

Baylor's eyebrows rose. Everyone knew who ran those businesses. The mafia. He didn't know how to feel. Chipper didn't give him time to think about it too much.

"You know, the Lunas are beautiful. I bet they have some amazing spots for wedding things—like pictures and receptions. Maybe even ceremonies. This is a great way for you to make a powerful connection."

In a house this huge, Baylor couldn't imagine running into Maverick's husband. If so, he didn't want to hijack Chipper's practice. "Maybe."

Chipper kissed his hand. "Thanks for coming with me."

"Of course." Baylor didn't even hesitate. "This is important to you. That makes it important to me."

Chipper cast a loving look Baylor's way that swelled his throat. He was everything Baylor's heart couldn't withstand. Or he wouldn't be exactly the healing balm Baylor hadn't wanted. It remained to be seen if there was any hope of fixing Baylor.

Humongous guards, in suits that cost as much as a car, opened their doors. They looked oddly friendly. Each smiled as they headed inside. Chipper held his hand the entire way. Even as accustomed to wealth as he was, Baylor couldn't stop looking in every direction. The place was gorgeous, but also so much more like a real home than it appeared to be from the outside. He swore he felt the way love lived there.

There was no one around as they came through the door. Chipper made his way through the house like he lived there. Finally, they reached an area that looked exactly like a professional ring. There were mats and even a cage. Workout equipment could be seen through a doorway. A glass case lined one wall. Awards gleamed on the other side. A huge guy greeted them.

He was all smiles as he pulled Chipper into a hug. "There he is. You're behind on shit. It's almost like you don't have an upcoming match." Despite the lecture, the man's honey-colored eyes looked much like a loving father's would. He cared about Chipper.

Baylor spoke up, hoping to take the heat in Chipper's stead. "That's my fault. I've been sick. He's been making sure I don't die."

Those gorgeous eyes turned his way. Maverick's smile didn't waver. "I heard." He held his hand out to Baylor. "Maverick."

Baylor accepted the handshake. "Baylor. It's nice to finally meet you."

"Same." Maverick focused on Chipper. "Get your ass in the ring and warm up. There're only so many hours in the day."

Chipper kissed Baylor's cheek, set his bag aside, and did as told.

Maverick made a sweeping gesture. "There's a chair over there, if you'd like to watch. If you get bored, feel free to explore." He chuckled. "If you get lost, you'll eventually run into someone."

Baylor's smile never dimmed. "Thanks, and thank you for understanding. Now, make sure he wins."

Maverick's smile grew. "Yes, sir."

Baylor liked his southern accent. He could listen to it all day, but he wanted Chipper to keep that title even more. He moved to a chair so they could get started. For the first few minutes, Baylor waffled between horrified by the powerful violence and impressed by Chipper's speed. He had seen Chipper work a bag, but this was different. Maverick was just as fast at blocking, but wow. He would not want to be on the receiving end of it. After the first ten minutes of repeated moves for training purposes, Baylor got a little bored. He had sat still more in the last few weeks than he ever had in his life. Baylor wasn't used to being still.

Despite Maverick saying he could explore, he hated to be too nosey. He moved to the nearby trophy case. He walked the line, inspecting various awards and belts. A new move caught Baylor's eye, pulling his gaze back to the cage. Almost too fast for the eye to see, Chipper landed a kick to the head, followed by a back kick on the opposite side. If Maverick hadn't been one of the best, the move definitely would have taken his head off.

"It's the trick move they've been perfecting for this upcoming fight. If Chipper can land it, he'll have the match in the bag."

Baylor turned his head and tried to hide the way the man's sudden appearance had startled him. He had been too engrossed to hear his approach. "I imagine so. That was impressive, yet terrifying."

A stoic nod met his words. "This is a brutal sport, but most people don't realize how much speed, power, and pure talent these men need. Like my husband, Chipper has all those things." He held his hand out. "I'm Zander."

Lord. He was beautiful. He was a zaddy. Goddamn. It was obvious Zander was much older than Baylor—likely in his fifties, but wow. Baylor accepted his handshake. "Baylor."

Zander dipped his chin. His light blue eyes were mesmerizing. His long blond hair tinged with gray caught the light and reflected it. He was expensive and polished. Yet he was also at home. He possessed a relaxed confidence Baylor wished he could achieve.

Baylor forced his gaze away and focused on the trophy case. He needed to find something else for his eyes to do. Thankfully, he spotted a gold medal. "Holy shit. Is that an Olympic medal?" He moved closer.

Zander moved with him. "Yes. Chipper has one too. I'm surprised you haven't seen it."

Baylor cocked his head and took a mental tour of Chipper's home. "You know, I don't think he has a single thing on display. I honestly don't know why I haven't noticed that before."

"Walk with me." Zander's hand landed on the small of Baylor's back. He allowed Zander to steer him from the room. As they left the workout equipment behind, exiting from a different door than where they entered, Baylor found himself surrounded by a jungle retreat. A waterfall gushed down a rock formation surrounded by lush greenery. It took Baylor a moment to spot the handholds and footholds. It was an obstacle course.

Before he embarrassed himself by exclaiming his shock, Zander snagged his whole attention. "I doubt Chipper's lack of displays has anything to do with him being humble. He simply has no one to see them."

Baylor looked his way. He fought the urge to point out that Chipper had him. Baylor understood Zander tried to lend his insight. "He knows absolutely everyone. It's a little crazy, actually. I've never seen anyone be friends with so many people around the country."

Zander flashed a sad smile. "Knowing people isn't the same as having people. He meets so many people because he never stops moving. If he stops, then he'll be forced to face an empty home. That's a feeling I understand. Silence can be..."

"Soul crushing," Baylor finished for him. "I know."

Zander held his stare. He was an odd mixture of scary, deep, and yet soothing. "I know you do. No one steps in my home I don't know. Since I knew it would only be a matter of time before Chipper brought you here, I had you investigated. Apologies for the intrusiveness, but I don't have the luxury of being any other way."

Baylor liked him. He was straightforward. Too few people were. "I'm unbothered. In my profession, as involved as I've been with dignitaries and celebrities, I imagine I've been investigated so many times, they have a file at the ready somewhere."

A huge grin lit Zander's face. "I did receive the information oddly fast."

Baylor laughed. "Ha. I knew it." His smile slipped. They had veered off topic and Baylor wanted whatever information Zander had about Chipper. "Chipper is exactly that: a chipper facade. He doesn't really show what's behind the mask. I've caught glimpses, but I get the feeling he has to hold tightly to that visage. Otherwise." Baylor shrugged.

Zander nodded. "He'd crack to pieces," Zander finished for him. He resumed walking and Baylor stayed in step. "You're the first person he's ever brought around. It's obvious you're special to him."

Baylor couldn't help the bright smile. "He's special to me too. That's something I never thought I'd say again."

"That's good to hear. He needs someone who actually sees him. Like you said, there's a real person behind the life of the party persona. For all his confidence in the cage, it's an act outside of it. People gravitate toward him, but only because he's a giver and people are users. When I learned about you, I hoped—for once—he'd found something and someone real. I see now, he has. He deserves to have someone give him back as much as he'll put in." He fell silent for a moment, leaving Baylor with his thoughts. Baylor had to find a way to be better for Chipper. Zander was right. Chipper deserved the world. "I heard you've been sick."

"Yeah." Even Baylor heard the defeat in his voice. "I've never been down this bad. They're saying something about my GFR and I have to see a nephrologist tomorrow. No matter how much rest I get, I don't feel any better. It's been a nightmare."

"Stay tonight. We have several private quarters. Chipper and you can relax, and I'd love for you to meet with my private physician. He's one of the best in the world. I feel certain he can put you at ease."

He didn't know what to say. Baylor got the feeling he couldn't say no. He also wasn't sure he wanted to decline. Someone like Zander would employ only the best of the best. "If Chipper doesn't mind, then that sounds fantastic. I really appreciate any insight other than the married doctor who tried to pick up Chipper the minute his wife turned her back."

Zander looked his way, obviously amused. "Don't stop there. This sounds like a story I need to hear."

Baylor laughed. He truly enjoyed himself way more than he expected. Without any hesitation, Baylor fell into the story of their disastrous appointment while they toured the house. It was a nice way to spend the afternoon and a stark reminder not to judge. He never expected to meet the head of the Russian mafia. Yet here he was, and the guy was awesome.

Chapter Eight

CHIPPER WATCHED BAYLOR EYE the clothes Zander's guards had found for him. Likely, Zander had sent them on a shopping spree. He looked content. For once, he didn't look ready to tear his hair out if he couldn't get back to work.

"I'm surprised you wanted to stay."

Baylor glanced up and smiled. "It was a nice day. Plus, Zander offered his physician. If he can make me feel better, I'm in." His gaze slid down Chipper's body like Chipper didn't still stink with sweat that molded his clothes to his skin. "I want to be back to a hundred percent so I can use it against you."

Whoa. His heated expression had Chipper's skin tingling. "I have strength to lend. You wouldn't have to do a thing except hold on."

"I'm in."

That caught Chipper off guard. He had only been letting Baylor know he was interested. Chipper had fully expected Baylor to laugh off his offer.

Baylor didn't stop there. "I could wash your back."

Chipper grabbed his bag. "I'd love that." He made his way to the bathroom and dropped his bag. After pressing a few buttons to get the shower going, Chipper dug out his small toiletries bag and placed it on the shelf inside the shower. He kept his mind busy in case Baylor didn't join him. Chipper didn't want to end up disappointed. As determined as he was to keep Baylor, he wasn't good at hanging on to people. There was something about him that people just couldn't love. He wished he knew what it was so he could change. He tried his ass off to be as good to everyone as possible. Obviously, he failed in some way.

Dark clouds gathered in his mind the more he went down that road. A nude Baylor stepped past him and into the shower. Like that, Chipper's mood cleared. A huge grin exploded across his face. Baylor didn't let him down. Chipper stripped out of his sweat-covered clothes. He wished he hadn't spent so much time brooding and more time showering before Baylor joined him. There was no way he would miss this, though.

Hot water hit Chipper from several directions as he climbed inside the shower. Baylor's face turned up toward the water. He slicked his hair back. Chipper let the water carry away some of the sweat before he molded against Baylor's back. "Goddamn. You're beautiful."

Baylor leaned into his touch. "I love the way you feel against me. That's probably an odd thing to say. It just feels good right here."

He got it. There was a peace when he held Baylor he couldn't explain. It was like he was finally whole and could rest. "It's not odd. Thoughts about holding you take up way more of my time than anything else." He kissed Baylor's shoulder. "I could stay exactly like this, never going further, and be happy. You've brought something to my life. I don't know exactly what it is, but I'm so fucking grateful."

A soft chuckle caressed his ears. "While I appreciate hearing that, I really want you inside me. Then I want you to hold me until this doctor comes."

He could do all that. "There's lube and a condom in that toiletries bag in front of you."

Baylor snagged the bag and handed things to Chipper as he needed them. They were methodical—like a team working together who had done this a million times. Chipper froze while lubing Baylor. He didn't want to be efficient, even though he recognized their actions showed how comfortable they were together. Chipper wanted chaos. He needed Baylor to feel as wanted as he was. Comfort aside, Chipper was crazy about Baylor. Baylor needed to know it.

Chipper snatched Baylor from his feet. With the slightest twist, he had Baylor's back against the wall with Baylor's sexy legs wrapped around his waist. The hunger and need written in Baylor's every line nearly buckled Chipper's knees. Comfortable or not, Baylor wanted Chipper. That was all Chipper needed.

"Hold on to me." He pushed his way inside, while watching Baylor's every reaction.

Baylor moaned like it was the first time anyone pleasured him. That could easily leave him addicted. His cheeks were flushed, and he looked as if he struggled for air. The visual alone threatened to push him over the edge. Baylor felt amazing. Chipper easily lifted and lowered while rolling his hips upward. Baylor weighed next to nothing. Chipper doubted Baylor made eating a priority. He would have to change that. Baylor would be so fucking spoiled. He couldn't tear his gaze away as he took Baylor. Baylor held his stare as if he felt the same.

"I was meant to be yours." Chipper didn't think he had ever uttered a truer sentence. "You completely own me."

A shaky-sounding breath filled the air. Baylor's green eyes seemed to turn even brighter. "Then come for me."

Chipper switched angles, ensuring he blew Baylor's mind. "You first." He thrust harder.

The back of Baylor's head hit the wall. He moaned and visibly fought for air. Chipper watched him strain toward release and thought he would lose his mind. He didn't know if he'd last. Chipper was right to worry. An orgasm ripped through him, stealing a loud cry from him. Thankfully, Baylor's cum filled the space between them, because Chipper couldn't even think, much less plot to make him blow. They kissed. It tasted like desperation. Chipper couldn't get close enough.

He didn't know which of them laughed first, but it started softly and grew. It was like happiness filled them until it boiled over and they couldn't contain it. Chipper let Baylor's feet hit the floor, but he didn't let go. He kissed Baylor's forehead, cheeks, chin, and nose. Chipper couldn't stop. He wanted to know he had kissed every inch of Baylor.

Baylor chuckled. "You're the biggest kid I know."

Chipper smiled against his cheek. "Maybe, but you like me."

"I do." Baylor's fingertips dug into Chipper's biceps. "I'm terrified I'll open my eyes any second and none of this will be real."

"It's real. Everything about us."

Baylor kissed him again, and Chipper forgot his plan to kiss every inch of Baylor. He could be happy with enjoying Baylor's tongue for now. They had forever for the rest.

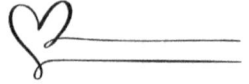

Baylor had no idea why his nerves fluttered so badly as he headed downstairs. It seemed the doctor had just arrived and would see him soon. Meeting new people didn't normally bother him. It was like this guy had the power to make or break him. That made zero sense, but he couldn't help his feelings. It was anxiety. He still hadn't fully gotten his meds back in his system yet.

Chipper squeezed his hand as they stepped into the sitting room. It was still empty. He chose a wingback chair near the door before his knees gave out.

"You'll love Dr. A. Zander flew him in from Florida. He doesn't trust anyone else as much."

"From Florida? For me? That has to be annoying."

"I don't mind. It's my job to make people better."

Baylor's gaze moved toward the voice. The air froze in his lungs. A guy with a perfectly pressed white coat and flawlessly styled brown hair stood in the doorway. In one hand, he carried an old time-y looking physician's bag. The other hand held the hand of a child. He looked to be the exact age Micah would be now if he lived. Baylor wondered if he would faint.

The guy smiled, looking every bit as great as Chipper claimed. "Hello. I'm Dr. A. You can also call me Corey if you'd like. I'm not picky." He lifted the boy's hand a bit. "I hope it's okay if my son joins us. My husband has whatever nasty virus is going around. I hear you know it well." He chuckled.

Baylor tried for a smile. His eyes wouldn't budge from the little boy. He wore a backpack and clutched a book against his chest. His eyes stayed carefully in a direction where no one was.

Corey motioned toward a nearby settee. "Why don't you sit over there while Dad works?"

With a sweet little nod that tore at Baylor's heartstrings, he headed for the couch.

Corey pulled a chair close to Baylor and opened his bag. He lowered his voice for Baylor's ears alone. "Seriously, I hope this is okay. Rhorey was adopted out of unthinkable conditions. He has special needs and can't be left alone with anyone else."

"It's fine." If only Baylor could breathe. "How old is he?"

"Eight."

"He's so tiny."

Corey flashed him a small smile. "Yeah. He came to us from a nightmare. Is it okay if I draw some blood? Zander says there's been a problem with your GFR. There's a lab onsite. I can have these tests running while we talk."

"That's fine." Baylor's gaze moved back to Rhorey.

Corey went to work, drawing several tubes of blood.

Baylor needed to focus on anything other than Rhorey's presence. "What does the A stand for?"

"Abayantsev. That was my last name before I married. I still call myself that when introducing myself to patients since that's the last name that's on my medical license."

That made sense. Baylor looked around, trying to keep his mind completely blank.

Rhorey suddenly stood and moved to Baylor's side. "I'm Rhorey." He spoke like an adult.

A sad smile tugged at Baylor's lips. "Hi, Rhorey. I'm Baylor."

He nodded and sat on Baylor's lap. "You're sad. I'll read you a book."

There was a knot in his stomach and a lump in his throat. He wanted to shove Rhorey from his lap. Worse, he wanted to wrap his arms around him and hold on so tightly he somehow brought Micah back to life. "Okay."

He felt the stillness in the air. Baylor glanced around. Everyone looked totally frozen. Corey visibly swallowed. He cleared his throat. "Sorry. Rhorey never lets anyone touch him other than a select few people he's known for years."

Rhorey opened his book. "It's okay. He's a daddy too."

Baylor immediately fought for air. He turned his head and blinked rapidly, trying not to fall apart.

Corey stared at him questioningly.

Baylor managed to breathe for half a second. "He passed away three years ago."

Corey looked truly upset on his behalf. "I'm sorry to hear that. There're no words."

Baylor gave a jerky nod.

Corey cleared his throat. "I have to run this to the lab. Come on, Rhorey."

Rhorey ignored Corey's outstretched hand. "He needs a story. When I was broken, Dada always read to me."

Before he knew it would happen, Baylor wrapped his arms around Rhorey and pulled him into a more comfortable position. Rhorey didn't complain.

"It's okay." When Baylor realized he said the words to himself, he focused on Corey so he wouldn't look crazy. "It's okay. We'll be okay."

While Corey still looked slightly unsure, he headed for the door.

Baylor focused on Rhorey and listened to him read. Each word was clear and concise. He had never met a kid like Rhorey. It was almost like he was an adult inside a child's body. Yet, he also seemed very fragile and young for his age. He was an enigma. Baylor had never been more curious about anyone. He couldn't be that nosey, though. Baylor would never dig for anyone else's trauma. Some things were better buried.

"What's your son's name?"

"Micah."

"How did he die?"

The question felt like it came from left field, but it didn't hurt as much coming from Rhorey. A child's curiosity was pure. "In a car accident."

Rhorey nodded. "I died once." He suddenly lifted his shirt, revealing a roadmap of horrible scars. It looked like someone had stabbed him repeatedly. He dropped his shirt. "My Dada saved me."

"It sounds like he loves you very much."

Rhorey smiled and bounced a little. "I got to ride in a plane on the way here. I mean, I get to do that all the time, but I got to watch them fly."

Baylor smiled. Kids' minds were so beautiful. "Do you like planes?"

Rhorey nodded. "I think I could fly one."

It took everything Baylor possessed not to laugh. It was obvious Rhorey truly believed he could just fly a plane. His jaw set in a hard line—almost like he dared someone to say otherwise.

"I believe in you."

A huge smile exploded across Rhorey's face.

Corey returned, still looking dumbfounded by Rhorey's reaction to Baylor. A massive man who looked more than a little scary was on his heels.

Rhorey scrambled from his lap. "Bear!"

The mountain kneeled and caught Rhorey as he ran into his arms. The guy wore a huge grin as he listened to Rhorey talk at a thousand miles an hour. He carried Rhorey away.

Corey didn't seem bothered, so Baylor assumed everything was fine. "I stayed until I got the results, since it only takes about five minutes." He reclaimed the chair at Baylor's side. His gaze moved between Baylor and Chipper and back again, reminding him Chipper had been there the whole time. Rhorey had flipped him on his head. Now he couldn't breathe for a whole new reason. Corey didn't look like a man about to deliver good news.

"With your permission, I'd like to do a nuclear GFR scan. A renal scan," he said, as if clarifying. "A small, thin plastic tube is inserted in the vein of your arm and a radioactive tracer is injected. The test takes about four hours, but it'll give me a clear picture of how your kidneys are actually functioning."

Chipper moved closer and took his hand.

Baylor's brow furrowed. "Why do we need that?"

Corey made a calming gesture at the slight panic in Baylor's tone. "My personal opinion is your kidneys are fine, but your bloodwork is wonky, and we need to rule that out. The numbers don't match. If you were dehydrated, I could tell. If your kidneys were diseased or failing, I could tell that too. Bloodwork is always the first and most important test anyone takes for anything. However, your blood doesn't show dehydration, disease, or failure. But your GFR is much lower than it should be."

"Why would that happen?"

At Chipper's question, his expression completely closed. While Baylor got the impression he didn't normally show emotion, he knew Corey held something back.

Baylor pressed. "Please. I swear you won't scare me. I'm just a worrier with high anxiety. If you don't tell me, I'll have a stroke."

A small smile played on Corey's lips at Baylor's dramatics. He shook his head. "When I drew your blood earlier, I noticed a few things." He took Baylor's arm and held it out. "You have a webbed pattern under the skin." Once Corey pointed it out, it was super obvious. It almost looked like hives were just under the skin, waiting to burst to the surface.

"What the hell!"

"And this." He turned Baylor's hand palm up and brushed the top of his finger down the tips of Baylor's. They were purple.

Now he was just confused as fuck. How had he not noticed that?

"There's also a hint of a rash across the bridge of your nose."

"I was in the sun yesterday."

Corey shook his head. "It's not a sunburn. I think you have lupus. I also think that's why you've been hit so hard by this virus and you're having such a hard time shaking it."

Chipper grabbed a chair and pulled it close to Baylor's side—like really getting into the conversation. "What are the options?"

Corey smiled. He looked kind. Baylor knew he must be to have saved Rhorey. "Let's not get ahead of ourselves. I took more blood than needed when I noticed the signs, but I don't have any results yet. Plus, I genuinely need to see what's happening with the kidneys. There're other possibilities such as blockages or lack of oxygen to the kidneys. We won't know for certain until I have all the results. If it is lupus, you'll be okay. I've obviously caught it really early if you haven't been completely hobbled by it before now or noticed the symptoms. That's a good thing. That means starting medications and getting ahead of things. No matter what we find, I'm glad Zander called. It takes years to get taken seriously in our health system and I'm better."

That might have sounded conceited, but Baylor got the feeling Corey had just saved him when an overworked nephrologist probably would've had to see him a thousand times before finding anything.

"Thank you. Whatever tests you need. I'm in."

Chipper kissed his temple and Baylor felt stronger than he had in a long time. It was strange that staring a challenge in the face was the thing he needed to breathe easier. Maybe that was a little of Rhorey's doing too, and a lot of Chipper's. Still, whatever happened, he wasn't quite as ready to leave this world yet as he was a month ago. He wasn't alone. That mattered more than anyone would ever know.

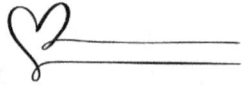

Chipper felt sick. He spent the evening hours searching for all the possibilities and treatments online. Baylor seemed oddly fine, and that worried him too. Chipper stopped pacing and rubbed his chest. Baylor's face when Rhorey called him a daddy. Something inside Chipper had shattered. He hurt all the way to his soul, and it wasn't even his son that was gone. No one could stand that close to that deep of a loss and walk away whole. It was a pain that scarred the universe. He had no clue how Baylor kept getting up every day. Chipper had to be his strength now.

"I was afraid I'd find you like this."

Chipper started at Maverick's sudden appearance. "Oh. Hey. Baylor is still getting scans. Apparently, this takes several hours."

Maverick nodded. "I know. That's why I'm here. I knew you'd be outside the door, wearing a hole in my floor."

A guilty smile snapped to Chipper's lips. He sat. "Sorry. I just don't handle medical shit very well."

Maverick nodded. "I know. PTSD from your mom."

He had to change the topic. "How did you know when you were ready to retire?"

Maverick blinked, obviously taken aback by the question. He sat. "Do you want to retire?"

Chipper shrugged. "I was just thinking about a conversation I had with Baylor. He asked what people did after losing their titles. It got me curious. You're the only person I know personally who's made it as far as I have. So how did you know you were done?"

Maverick leaned back in his seat. "Zander. He always came to every fight. I knew his would be the last face I saw before stepping into the cage and the first face I'd look for when I won. My final match, my gaze immediately found him as soon as it ended. I looked at him and I chose him. It suddenly hit me how many hours, days, weeks I'd spent training. That was time away from him for a ten-second match that meant abso-fucking-lutely nothing. Don't get me wrong. It was everything at one point, but not really, because he's really what's always been everything. In a flash of clarity, I wanted those moments back I lost trying to be the best."

"To be fair, for most of us, it's longer than ten seconds in the ring."

Maverick laughed. "Even the matches that lasted longer than that weren't worth the time I lost. It's just a sport. I love it and I'll probably never totally walk away. After all, Zander has shit to do during the day that doesn't involve me, but I don't want to split my focus anymore. I choose him."

"I figured it was something like that."

The door to the medical center inside Zander's home opened. Corey stepped out. "I'm just running an IV of saline through Baylor to make sure I flush all the dye from his system. Plus, he's a bit dehydrated now.

Thankfully, though, his kidneys look to be functioning perfectly, exactly as I expected."

Relief flooded through Chipper

"Unfortunately, it's as I suspected. He has lupus. I've run the bloodwork several times. He has all the markers, and he's had more symptoms than he realized. He said he works so much, he didn't notice."

"That sounds about right," Chipper muttered under his breath. "How is he holding up after the news?"

Corey motioned toward the door. "You can go see for yourself if you'd like." Chipper took a step toward the door and Corey stopped him. He looked expressionless, as always, but there was something dark in his eyes. "I'm sorry if Rhorey triggered Baylor. I've never seen Rhorey act like that with a stranger and I honestly didn't know the right way to handle things."

Chipper thought about Baylor's every reaction. "Honestly, I think it helped in some way. Right before you came back, Rhorey asked about Micah, and it was the first time I've seen him talk about his son without falling apart. I think he needed that."

Corey nodded. "Rhorey is an old soul. He has an uncanny ability to help others."

"Sounds like he ended up with the right family, then."

Corey smiled. "I'll let you go see Baylor now, and I have a bedtime story to read."

Chipper dipped his chin. "Thank you for everything. I know we took you away from your husband when he needs you."

Corey laughed. Chipper didn't think he had ever seen him genuinely laugh. "Rhett? He hates anyone seeing him sick and it would kill him if Rhorey caught something from him. You know he's a giant puppy."

Chipper snorted and headed in to see Baylor. He had no idea what he would find with the way the night had gone.

Baylor looked up from his spot on the bed as Chipper came through the door. He looked fine. "Hey."

Chipper moved to sit on the edge of the bed. "Hey. How are you feeling?"

Baylor shrugged. "Fine. How are you feeling?"

Chipper couldn't help but smile. Baylor shouldn't be worried about him. "Worried about you."

Baylor scooted over and patted the bed. "Come here. Cuddle with me."

In five seconds, Chipper had Baylor in his arms. He didn't need to be asked twice to do his favorite thing.

As soon as he was settled, Baylor kissed his chest. "I really am fine. Corey talked to me about treatment. It's just a bunch of meds. That's no big deal. Everything else will come as it comes. But apparently, since I'll be medicated, this isn't life-threatening. I'll just have to be extra careful to not catch anything." He paused for a second. Chipper practically heard the wheels turning in his head, coming to grips with all the ramifications. "I suppose I need to slow down."

Chipper tried to keep the happiness from his voice. He truly wanted Baylor to stop killing himself, but he hadn't known how to make it happen. It was better for Baylor to make the decision on his own. "Have you started working on a plan? I know you're booked solid for like the next two years."

Baylor tilted his head back to meet Chipper's stare. "How would you know that?"

He pointed at himself. "Stalker. Remember? I've had to finagle a lot of wedding invitations to see you."

"I fucking knew it!" Baylor covered his mouth as if he hadn't meant to shout. His eyes swam with laughter. He dropped his hand. A huge smile played on his lips. "I knew there was no way you go to that many weddings all the time."

Chipper couldn't stop smiling. "Of course it was all for you. Everything is these days."

Baylor looked moved... and happy.

He couldn't resist pointing that out. "For someone who just got life-altering news, you look strangely elated."

He felt Baylor shrug. "I don't know why it doesn't look that daunting right now, but it doesn't." Baylor seemed to turn inward for a moment before his gaze locked on Chipper again. "That's not true. I know why. Meeting you has turned my world upside down in all the best ways. I can't explain it, but I feel like... It's stupid."

"Nothing you say could be stupid."

Baylor visibly swallowed. "I feel like I won't ever be alone again."

That was exactly how they felt to him too. They had something big. Something life-altering. From the outside looking in, it had to look like they were two idiots who didn't really know each other, but they did. He couldn't explain it. Maybe it was due to

Chipper caring for Baylor through an illness. He didn't think so, though. They just found something in each other. Something they were both missing.

He kissed Baylor. "You won't be." Their kiss was so sweet, it sent a flutter through Chipper's chest. He held Baylor tighter and savored every second. He had never been so full.

Chapter Nine

THE CROWD WAS SO damn loud. Chipper couldn't focus on that, or the nerves would set in. Instead, he let Baylor rule his mind. He fought a smile so he didn't look like an idiot sitting there smiling like a crazy person. Things had been damn good since Chipper chased him from Bandit's place. He hadn't left Chipper's house or bed. It was like they silently agreed Baylor lived there now. Baylor had started his treatment and passed an ass-ton of work to Sacha. Thankfully, he also hired two additional people so Sacha wouldn't drown. His one-man operation had quickly become a company supporting employees. Chipper would gladly help pay a few salaries if Baylor would stay home. There was a lot Baylor could still do without personally showing up at every venue. In fact, the only venue he had visited in the past few weeks had been the one they were renting for Eric's birthday. That was fine since it wasn't far, and Chipper got to go along. He knew he would have to let Baylor out of his sight eventually. Maverick was right, though. Chipper had some PTSD from the way his mom died.

"It's time." Maverick looked serious.

"Is Bay here?"

Maverick gave him a sharp nod. "Right up front. He's with Zander."

That was all Chipper needed to hear. With a quick nod, Chipper's jaw set. He fell into work mode. His mind emptied as he went through final inspections. People chanted his name. All Chipper saw was Baylor. He held Chipper's stare, looking completely confident. At the cue, Chipper headed inside the cage. At the last second, he looked Baylor's way again and winked. Baylor's smile made everything feel lighter.

He listened to the rules. There weren't many. He stared down the man who wanted this every bit as badly as Chipper did. Chipper got it. He had once been the guy determined to snag the title. There was one thing Chipper had that he didn't. Baylor waited for him.

The bell rang. His opponent immediately threw a punch. Chipper didn't think. He reacted. He dodged and then pulled his trick move. Chipper hadn't planned to try it this early in the match, but the wild swing—likely due to nerves—left the perfect opening. Chipper unleashed a spin kick, landing solidly before the other heel also collided. Before he fully accepted what happened, Chipper's arm was raised in victory. The crowd was so loud, he couldn't hear. He blinked at the guy on the mat, being looked over by a medical team. Chipper knew he would be good. They were built to take hits. Then, just as Maverick had described, his gaze automatically sought Baylor. A smile exploded across his face when he saw Baylor cheering for him. Ignoring the officials trying to run through the usual title announcement, he walked to the wire fence separating him from his heart. The announcers screamed into the microphone, trying to keep the crowd pumped so they didn't feel like they wasted two hundred dollars to watch a fight end in seconds.

Chipper had to yell over the noise. "I choose you."

Baylor looked confused. "What?"

"I choose you," he yelled louder.

Baylor didn't look any less confused, but he yelled back. "I love you too."

Chipper's heart stopped for a second. Somehow, his smile got even bigger. He would take it. Chipper would absolutely take those words over any response Baylor could have given if he had understood Chipper's words.

He let someone pull him away to do what needed to be done. But Chipper walked backward and never looked away from Baylor. Baylor had said he loved him. That was the biggest prize he had ever won in his life. He got it now. Chipper understood what waited for him on the other side of this career. It was love and family. Baylor deserved a happy home and children. Fuck, he wanted everything with Baylor. He didn't care how long they had known each other. They knew each other. Baylor was the realest thing to ever happen to him. He wasn't alone anymore, and he wasn't scared of what would happen next. Chipper had found his home.

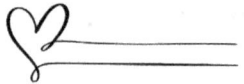

Damn. Chipper looked sexy as hell. Larger than life. He only had eyes for Baylor. It was the hottest moment of his life. He could barely breathe while he watched Chipper go through the ceremony of hanging on to his title. Goddamn. That had been hot too. Chipper had landed that trick move perfectly. His opponent had hit the floor so fast, it had taken Baylor a second to realize he had been knocked out. He wondered if this was some sort of record. It was definitely badass. His man had done that. But the way Chipper looked at him now, that was... wow. Chipper had said he loved him in front of thousands of people. The pride he felt couldn't be contained, but it also had nowhere to go.

After what felt like ages, Chipper stepped from the cage. He expected it would still be a while before they were together. He had ridden to the arena with Zander so they could all leave the arena together. Zander's driver had dropped off Maverick and Chipper earlier in the day for all the pre-match bullshit that obviously took forever.

"Come on." Zander took his arm and started the push toward the aisle. "I can get us in the back."

Baylor practically danced in place with impatience. It turned out he didn't have to wait. While he had his head down, ensuring he didn't step on anyone, Chipper appeared from nowhere and snatched him off his feet. His mind had a hard time reconciling, going from trying to get to Chipper to being over Chipper's shoulder as he made his way to the back of the building. People shouted and cellphone cameras pointed their way. Security stayed tight knit around them. Maverick and Zander followed with what looked to be a private security team. He recognized two of the men. One had driven them to the arena, and the other had ridden in the back with them. Sometimes he forgot Zander was a big deal. Baylor had to focus on anything except his current position. In minutes, photos of him ass up would be all over the internet. At least they had gotten his good side.

Chipper didn't set him on his feet until they were inside a locker room. It was huge—like it was normally used by the professional hockey team in the area, which made sense since this was their arena. It looked as if it had been reserved for only Chipper.

Baylor bounced in place. "You did it! I'm so proud of you."

Chipper looked so damn proud. Baylor loved him so much. He didn't know why they hadn't admitted it before now. Chipper hugged him so tightly, he couldn't breathe. He didn't care. Chipper kept one arm around Baylor while he clapped hands and shook with everyone congratulating him. Maverick and Zander got hugs. The praise seemed never ending, especially for the winning move he had worked so hard to perfect. While Baylor was over-the-top proud and excited, he selfishly couldn't wait until he had Chipper to himself.

Chipper dressed while everyone talked. It looked like it would be a while before they celebrated alone. Baylor got it. Everyone was excited. Maverick had worked his ass off with Chipper, and Zander had sacrificed time with his husband.

"Visitor coming."

At the loud announcement, Baylor's gaze snapped to the doorway. Chipper's opponent strolled inside, already dressed in street clothes. An inner groan ran through Baylor's head. Baylor thought the guy's name was Tip. He was all smiles, which confused Baylor.

Chipper met him halfway. They shook hands and hugged. They spoke for a while, out of earshot. Only briefly did Tip stop smiling. Then he simply nodded, looking like he hung on every word Chipper said. Baylor was curious as hell.

Maverick followed his gaze. "MMA is a family. Chipper understands how badly the kid wanted this. We all do. We've all been him. It just wasn't his night. There are no hard feelings, but he needs to hear Chipper tell him he can still do it."

Every day, Baylor was more impressed with Chipper. He was such a great guy. It hurt Baylor's chest to think of all the time he spent alone, no one seeing beyond the fighter. Baylor hated he could be counted among those numbers once.

"You really love him."

Baylor glanced Maverick's way at the comment. "I do."

Maverick looked serious. He gave a sharp nod. "Good. I'm glad to hear it. It's been hard watching him win time after time and then go home to an empty house. Success isn't enough to sustain anyone."

Baylor nodded. "That I definitely know."

Before they could say anything more, Chipper returned. He grabbed Baylor around the waist and kissed him several times on the forehead until Baylor couldn't stop smiling.

Zander stepped in. "Unless you have some burning desire to go out and celebrate, we'll escort you safely home, so you can savor your win privately."

Baylor refused to look at Chipper and let him see his desperation to go home. The way he chose to celebrate his win needed to be his decision. "I appreciate that. Baylor and I have a lot to talk about."

Wow. Chipper knew he had anxiety. He wouldn't make it until they got home. Baylor snagged two handfuls of Chipper's shirt and pulled him down for a quick kiss. While he had him, he kissed his ear and then kept his words between them. "You know I can't handle a let's discuss this later moment."

Chipper kissed his cheek. "It's okay, baby. I just need your advice."

Baylor released him. He could handle that. His heart rate slowed. He linked his fingers through Chipper's and headed toward whatever Chipper needed from him. He wouldn't let him down. Still, despite Chipper's claim, a hint of nervousness grew on the ride home. Zander's guard, Yaro, drove. Chipper spent the trip constantly stealing kisses. He didn't think Chipper had any plans of kicking him to the curb or anything. He worried about Chipper. It wasn't like Chipper to have too many overly serious conversations. He was a big child, and that was one of the many things Baylor loved about him.

Yaro steered into the driveway.

Baylor spoke up. "Why don't you all join us for a single toast before heading home?"

Chipper didn't argue.

Baylor breathed an inner sigh of relief. They all piled from the SUV and headed for the door. Baylor subtly fell slightly behind Chipper as he unlocked the front door. The lights automatically flared to life at the motion of the door swinging open.

"Surprise!" The shout was deafening.

Chipper's expression was completely worth the scrambled work it had taken to pull together as many of Chipper's friends as possible in a short time. Thankfully, he was the king of party planning. Chipper's shocked gaze turned his way.

Baylor beamed.

"What if I had lost?" Chipper sounded floored—like he didn't know what else to say.

"I knew you wouldn't."

He was engulfed by people congratulating him. They filed inside and champagne glasses filled their hands.

Sacha wrapped his arm around Baylor's waist and swept him aside. He kissed Baylor's cheek. "You did great, babe. He looks like you could knock him over with a feather."

Baylor wrapped his arm around Sacha too. "It's all thanks to you and your hard work."

Sacha scoffed. "Please. All I did was make sure the vendors got here on time, and the buses picked up guests from the parking lot we rented. You did every ounce of the real work."

Baylor had to because it was for Chipper. Everything had to be perfect. It was worth it to see his expression. For once, the party was for only him. He didn't have anyone to celebrate him. Baylor wanted the job. He didn't forget Sacha's part or how the guy worked his ass off for him. "Still, you're amazing. You have a salary increase coming on your next check."

Sacha looked his way with raised eyebrows. "You just raised my salary when you took a step back."

Baylor shrugged. "The work you do should always be properly compensated. You're loved and appreciated. I want you to always know it."

Sacha squeezed him. "Awww. You're loved too."

Bandit appeared with more champagne. "This turned out amazing. Of course, my two favorite people pulled it off, so of course it turned out perfect."

Sacha blushed and accepted the fresh glass.

Baylor eyed the pair on the sly. He knew Sacha had a huge crush on Bandit. Sacha didn't hide it very well. The thing was, Bandit had always been an oblivious idiot. He never recognized when people liked him. Baylor didn't know how to help things along or if he should. They were his friends. If things went south, he would be stuck in the middle. Still, he felt good about love tonight.

"Oh. Do you two think you could do the honors of wheeling out the cake? I don't think I trust anyone else to get it in here safely."

Sacha didn't hesitate. "Of course."

Baylor kissed his cheek again. "Then I guess I should face the firing squad about allowing over a hundred people in Chipper's house without him knowing." He laughed as he walked away, but he actually was a little nervous. Chipper looked happy, but Baylor lived with a constant sense of dread in the back of his mind. He knew that was trauma and PTSD, but he was who he was. Now, he needed to see if it was warranted.

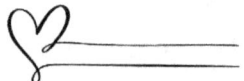

Discomfort settled in the moment Baylor walked away. Bandit had always taken Sacha a little off kilter. He was accustomed to being the most confident person in the room. Bandit was different from everyone else he dealt with. He was a strange mixture of too serious and yet silly. Sacha couldn't explain it. It was almost as if he stayed at war with himself, and Sacha didn't know what battle he fought.

Their gazes met. His unique blue eyes always caught his attention and held it. They looked so strange with his bright red hair and freckles. Sacha had actually looked up the stats. Blue eyes with red hair were the rarest combination in the world. Sacha wanted to ask how he had turned out this way—like the guy would know. He was tall and lanky—just like Sacha. Sacha always thought they would look good together. It was just wishful thinking. Bandit only thought of Sacha as Baylor's employee. He might as well not exist.

Bandit motioned toward the dining room, where the cake waited. "Shall we?"

Sacha tore his gaze away and headed in the direction he'd indicated. He would keep his head down and this gigantic cake safe.

This was his job, and Bandit was Baylor's oldest and closest friend. The dining room light was off, hoping to deter people from wandering in. He had marked the room as off limits, but people never thought signs applied to them.

Sacha flipped on the lights.

"Whoa!" Bandit set his champagne glass aside and circled the cake, inspecting it. "Holy shit. This is cake? It's amazing."

Sacha twisted his fingers and stared at the intricate design. It was a cage surrounding an MMA ring. There was a tiny guy inside with his arms lifted in victory. He had also made one that was two fighters shaking hands. He planned to quickly switch them out if Chipper lost. Sacha hadn't told Baylor that. "Do you really like it? I made it."

Bandit's chin shot up. He held Sacha's stare. "You did this? Seriously?"

Sacha nodded. "My cake designs are how I met Baylor. He hired me to make a wedding cake and everything kind of took off from there. The entire thing is edible."

Bandit shook his head and eyed the cake again. "Damn. I hate for it to get eaten. It's too awesome."

Sacha couldn't stop smiling. He didn't get to design cakes very often any longer. It was his biggest passion. He missed it. Bandit's praise filled his chest with warmth. "Thank you. This was the one dream I had for myself."

Bandit watched him like he saw too much. "Why aren't you doing it, then?"

Sacha shrugged. "It isn't the dream that came true. This position with Baylor is the next best thing and pays way more than I ever thought I would make. It definitely pays better than making cakes ever would. The economy beat me," he added with a nervous chuckle. No one ever asked about his dreams.

"You never know. Life has a way of leading you exactly where you're meant to be. I think you were meant for this." He motioned toward the cake. "You're not given this much talent for nothing."

He was so fantastic. It hurt Sacha's chest a little. While it was one thing to have a small, secret crush, it was a whole other to see him like this—flawlessly supportive. "Thank you. Maybe it'll happen someday."

Bandit's gaze never wavered from Sacha. "I believe in you."

Fuck his life. Sacha was a goner.

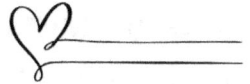

To say Chipper rode cloud nine would be the understatement of a lifetime. Hell, he was on cloud twenty-nine—a type of cloud that hadn't even been discovered yet. It was all due to Baylor. He thought he would scream before the final guests finally left. Chipper closed the door behind Zander and his bunch and leaned against it. He held Baylor's stare.

"I can't believe you did this."

Baylor shifted from foot to foot. "You deserve to be celebrated."

Damn. He wanted to shout his happiness at the top of his lungs. "This is the most amazing thing anyone has ever done for me."

"You matter to me."

Chipper crossed the distance between them and hauled Baylor into his arms. He squeezed him against his chest. "You make me stupidly happy." He had so many things he wanted to say to Baylor. Chipper didn't know where to start.

Baylor kissed his chest. "You said you needed to talk to me about something, which almost made me regret this party. This has been the longest fucking night, waiting to hear what you have to say."

He kissed the top of Baylor's head. Chipper kind of regretted saying anything at the arena. He knew Baylor had anxiety.

"I'm sorry." He led Baylor to the couch. Rather than sit next to him, he towed Baylor into his lap. He took a deep breath once they were settled. "I think I'm done."

Baylor's every muscle froze. "You told me not to worry!"

Chipper realized how he sounded and rushed to fix it. "With fighting, baby. I think tonight was my last bout."

Baylor didn't relax much. He looked one part horrified and three parts like he didn't know what to say. "Why?"

Chipper's shoulders relaxed at the question. For whatever reason, when Baylor questioned him, Chipper felt safe to pour out his heart. He had never had this—a real place to land. "In a way, it goes back to what we talked about that night when you were in the tub. For a while now, I've stressed hard over failing and what I would do when I did. Tonight, when I realized I'd won, it also hit me why it scared me so badly to lose. Until now, I've literally had nothing else that mattered to me. I've kept going because it's not like I had a life to come home to. MMA is the only family I've had since my mom passed. I've been exhausted for a long time, but I didn't know how to quit just to spend the rest of my life alone."

Chipper brightened. He never stayed sad for long and he held Baylor. That made it twice as hard to feel down. "But the moment I turned and saw you, waiting and cheering for me, I knew I could stop. I have something better at home."

Baylor's eyes were filled with tears.

Chipper panicked a bit. "Was I wrong? I guess I shouldn't have assumed."

Baylor kissed him, cutting off the anxiety-filled flow of words. He gently held Chipper's face. He may as well have had Chipper in a headlock. Chipper couldn't move. Baylor's tongue brushed his in the sweetest of motions. Chipper's heart soared through the roof.

Baylor pulled away and brushed noses with him. "I love you. God knows, it's probably crazy, but I do. Being with you is healing me in ways I never thought could happen. If I'm doing the same for you in some small way, then thank God I'm not alone." He touched his forehead to Chipper's and took a deep breath. It sounded ragged. "I know this isn't the time to do or say this, but I have to leave town for a couple of days tomorrow."

Chipper jerked backward. "Why? Can it wait for one day? I have to do a few interviews tomorrow, but the next day, I could go with you anywhere." That would be one benefit of retiring. There was no reason he couldn't always travel with Baylor.

"Just trust me this one time. This is something I need to do alone."

Damn. When Baylor put it like that, he couldn't balk too much. "But I'll miss you." He knew he sounded childish. Chipper didn't care. He had made this huge life decision, and he wanted Baylor at his side.

"I'm sorry. If this wasn't important to me, I'd never do this to you. I promise it'll be the last time we're apart."

Chipper pressed his forehead against Baylor's again and nodded, squishing foreheads with him. "Okay." He sounded exactly like a petulant child.

"Tonight, I plan to suck your dick."

Chipper immediately brightened. "Okay."

Baylor stood and took Chipper's hand. Chipper followed him down the hall with his heart in his throat. Maybe he didn't show it, but loving Baylor scared the shit out of him. He was hyper aware he might never measure up to Freddie. Chipper wanted them to have their own version of a happy life. Freddie was the one thing Chipper worried would keep that from happening. He didn't know how to lose this.

Chapter Ten

THE PLANE RIDE WAS rough as hell. Baylor held himself together by sheer will alone. Since he rented a car for the last leg of his journey, Baylor was free to fall apart a little. Chipper planned to retire to be with him. He knew that wasn't the whole of it, but their relationship had been the thing that tipped the scales. Chipper planned to officially give their relationship his all. He deserved the same energy. Baylor didn't know how to do that if he couldn't make peace with the past. That was why Baylor had to try.

He sat in his rental, staring at nothing for much longer than necessary. Only the knowledge he had to do this made him step from the car. It was the first time since their funeral that Baylor had come here, but he still knew exactly where to find their graves among the countless headstones. Bandit had paid to put a concrete bench next to them. Baylor guessed Bandit thought he was braver than he was and would visit all the time. This place was his personal hell. He didn't want to be here.

Still, Baylor found the bench and sat. Despite his best efforts, his gaze wouldn't meet his babies' names carved forever in stone. Baylor blew out a breath. He wasn't sure he would ever stop feeling like he would die. The pain was that big. But he truly had fallen in love again with a good man who deserved to have as much of him as possible.

"God, I miss you. You were so easy to talk to. Before I met you, I don't think I'd ever taken a full breath. I walked on the eggshells of a terrible childhood. You were everything I'd never known. You gave me a beautiful child." Baylor's voice shook. He had to take a few breaths before trying again. "Losing you two just proved every belief I ever had that I didn't deserve love, but now there's this guy." An unexpected bark of laughter burst from him. "I guess you know that, though." Baylor swiped the tears from his cheeks. "Did you do this?" He whispered the question, feeling crazy. "Did you send him to me? You two are so much alike. He's big and goofy as hell. I guess you knew that too since you two have met." Baylor sat in silence for a moment, trying to find the words he needed so badly to say before starting again. "There will never come a day when I don't miss you both." Another shaky breath escaped him. "But I have to move on before this hole in my chest kills me. I'm pretty sure it almost happened not that long ago, but Chipper pulled me away from the edge. Now I can't stop thinking about how he's where I belong now." He leaned over, getting close to Freddie's grave. Baylor lowered his voice to a whisper again. "You know me. I'm about to do something really crazy that'll make everyone question my sanity. But following my heart gave me the best years of my life with you two. Now I have to see if I can create a few more." He kissed his fingers and touched the ground. "I love you guys."

Baylor walked away. He still had a few things he wanted to do while he was in town before he flew home. Home. He hadn't had one of those in a long time. Chipper had given that back to him. Baylor had to do the same for him. He just didn't know yet if he could

Baylor drove aimlessly for a while, trying to decide if he felt better or worse. Finally, he stopped at a tiny cafe Freddie would take him to when they were in town. They didn't have a huge menu, but Baylor ordered something. He was beginning to learn his triggers for flare-ups and not eating was one. Baylor didn't want to feel any worse than he already did. As he waited for the order, Baylor sat in a booth and went back to staring after nothing. His mind raced too hard for him to keep up.

"Baylor!"

Baylor turned his head at the sound of the child's voice in just enough time to have a body launched at him. A smile exploded across his face as Rhorey's tiny arms wrapped around his neck. "Oh. Hey, sweetie. Where did you come from?"

"Rhorey. Oh my God. I'm so sorry. You must remind him of someone."

Rhorey took up the spot next to him, obviously having no interest in leaving.

Baylor focused on the man apologizing. His brain lagged, making him slow to explain because, goddamn. The guy was hands down the most beautiful man Baylor had ever seen. He was the definition of stunning. He fucking stunned words right out of Baylor. A blond Adonis. Fuck.

Thankfully, Rhorey had him. "It's Baylor, Dada. We met at Uncle Zander's."

Relief washed over his face. "Oh. Thank God. It's nice to meet you. Rhorey talked about you for days after you two met."

Baylor smiled. How could anyone not while in his presence? "Please have a seat. You must be Corey's husband."

They shook hands. "Rhett." Rhett sat across from him.

"Oh. How cute. Rhett and Corey, Rhorey."

Rhett was all smiles like sunshine in a bottle. He offset Corey's serious nature perfectly. Damn. Corey had torn himself away from this to help Baylor. He was twice as grateful now.

"I thought you lived in California."

Baylor nodded. His throat swelled. "I do. This was my husband's hometown. He and my son are buried here. I came to see them."

The genuine hurt that touched Rhett's features nearly made Baylor burst into tears. He took Baylor's hand. "I'm so sorry. We almost lost Rhorey. I can't even imagine."

He never knew what to say when people told him how sorry they were, but he was thankful for Rhett, nonetheless. While Rhett might not have lost his son, Baylor gathered he had gotten close enough to understand in a way most people didn't.

"He's not here."

Baylor took his hand back from Rhett and put his arm around Rhorey. "Who's not here, honey?"

"Micah." He made a wild motion with his hand, as if drawing a picture he saw in his mind. "He went somewhere else." He returned to the coloring book he had pulled out while Baylor had been talking to Rhett. Rhorey didn't look his way. "When I died, I went away too. I was happy and didn't want to come back. Not until I heard Dada's voice."

While Baylor wasn't sure if any of this was true, he was fascinated.

Then Rhorey turned his head. His blue eyes were so serious, Baylor knew he never made up stories. It was as if life had made him too mature for that nonsense. He held Baylor's stare. "He doesn't want you to be sad."

Baylor swallowed. Tears slipped down his cheeks and there was no stopping it. He swiped at them, trying to show some self-control in front of a child who should never shoulder an adult's trauma.

"It would hurt." Rhorey touched his chest. "Right here, if my dads cried. He doesn't want that."

Baylor took a breath and tried to pull himself under control. "Okay. I'll try."

With a nod, Rhorey returned to coloring. His gaze automatically swung Rhett's way. He didn't look surprised.

He gave Baylor a sweet smile. "Listen to the boy. He got Corey's genius."

Baylor chuckled. "And his compassion from you, I'm betting. Would you like to join me for dinner? I already ordered, but I'd love the company."

"Sure. Corey is in the car, giving night orders to his nursing staff. He'll be in as soon as he's done. I'm sure he'd love to see you."

Rhorey took his hand under the table and held it. A peace settled over Baylor he hadn't felt in years. When Rhorey had first appeared at his table, he had mused over how small the world was. Now he saw the truth. Too many blatant signs pointed him toward this new path. Baylor was doing the right thing. He could go home now.

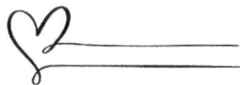

Chipper hated sleeping without Baylor. He tossed and turned, beating the pillow next to him, attempting to make it more Baylor-like. Nothing worked. He was miserable. At two a.m., he gave up and got up. He headed for the kitchen. Chipper would eat another slice of the amazing cake Baylor had gotten him. He got one bite in and heard the front door chirp, then the beep of the alarm being reset. Chipper picked up his plate and headed for the living room. He wasn't too worried. Anyone who knew his alarm code wasn't likely set on killing him. His heart soared at the sight of Baylor parking his suitcase against the wall.

"Hey, baby."

Baylor jumped, and then bent at the waist, sucking air. "Holy shit, Chipper. You scared the shit out of me. Why are you up?"

"Couldn't sleep." He couldn't stop smiling. "Sorry about scaring you. I didn't think you'd be home for a couple of days."

Baylor straightened and gave him a sweet smile. "I couldn't stay away. I missed our bed." His gaze lowered to Chipper's plate. "But I see you found a way to entertain yourself."

Chipper looked down at the humongous slice of cake on his plate. "What? My bout is over. I don't have to restrict myself anymore." He cocked his head and thought it over. "Maybe I should still watch it, though. You're naturally a small guy. I don't think you'd like it if I got fat."

Baylor chuckled as he crossed the room. "First off, you as a bear daddy. Mmm. Yum. Secondly, I don't know that I'm naturally small as much as I was just starved as a kid." He stole a kiss.

Chipper had learned Baylor didn't say things, digging for pity. He was just straightforward. "Do you want a piece of cake too? I'd never let you go hungry."

Baylor eyed his plate. "Can I just have a bite of yours?"

Chipper huffed. "You know damn well you want more than one bite."

Baylor's serious expression never wavered. It was like this was an important decision for him. "Can I have yours if I fix you another slice?"

He had no clue why it mattered, but he didn't care. Chipper shrugged. "Sure."

They headed for the kitchen.

Chipper sat while Baylor moved around the kitchen, getting out a second plate.

"Do you plan to tell me where you went?"

"I went to see Freddie and Micah."

Chipper assumed he meant their graves. "Okay. You could've just said that. I would've understood."

Baylor worked with his back to Chipper. "I know, but I needed to talk to them. Work some things out in my head."

Chipper wasn't so sure he wanted any more cake. They were back to him, feeling inferior. His appetite vanished. He would never let Baylor see that. It wasn't Baylor's fault he felt insecure. Chipper had known the score going in. "Did it help you work things out?"

"No. Rhorey did, though."

Chipper's eyebrows shot up. It was taking Baylor forever to slice a single piece of cake. Chipper wanted him to sit down and talk to him. "Rhorey? Where in the hell did you see Rhorey?"

Baylor laughed. "I know. The world is small as hell. When Corey said he lived in Florida, I had no idea he meant the same small-ass town Freddie was born in. That's where he's buried," Baylor explained unnecessarily. He turned with a plate in hand and swapped plates with Chipper. "Oh. It gets better. It turns out Rhett's first year of teaching at the high school, Freddie was in his class."

"Damn. You met the pretty boy, huh?"

Baylor blinked, as if he had no idea what Chipper meant.

Chipper pulled a disbelieving face. "Come on, now. I've seen the guy. You don't have to hold back."

A smile exploded across Chipper's face as Baylor broke. "Holy hell. Why is he so pretty? It's unnatural. I can't even imagine Corey meeting him. Not that I don't think Corey could get someone like him. It's just Corey is so serious."

"He's autistic."

"Oh." Baylor looked thoughtful for a second. "That explains a lot, actually. But still, Corey must've been fucking dying inside when Rhett looked his way."

Chipper knew this story. He didn't mind regaling Baylor with the tea. "Well, see..." Chipper's voice died as he dropped his gaze to his plate to take a bite. It had a ring sticking out of the top. His chin lifted. His brain refused to work.

Baylor stood and moved to his side. He dropped to one knee. "Will you marry me? People will think we're nuts, but I learned a very important lesson three years ago. Life can be ripped away from you at any moment. Waiting when you really want something is stupid. It might not be there tomorrow. So what do you say? Want to do something completely crazy with me and get married?"

Chipper couldn't fucking believe it. He definitely thought he would have to beg for years to convince Baylor to take that big of a risk on him. He was blown away. Chipper wanted to ask if he was fucking with him, but he wasn't that dumb. He knew Baylor would never do this unless he was a hundred percent sure. "Yeah. I want that more than anything." He snatched Baylor off the floor and stood, squeezing him and stealing kisses. Baylor wrapped his legs around him and held on every bit as tightly.

"I love you." He kissed Baylor hard. "Goddamn. I love you so fucking much."

"I love you too." Baylor forced him to soften, leading him into a sweet kiss. When Chipper couldn't handle it anymore, he threw Baylor over his shoulder.

"Hey. I actually wanted that cake."

Chipper put his ring in his mouth and sucked it clean as he grabbed his plate with the bigger piece and headed down the hall. He would personally feed his soon-to-be husband. Fuck. He hoped Baylor wanted all the bells and whistles. Chipper wanted the whole world to know Baylor was his. He tossed Baylor on the bed and set the cake on the bedside table. With his hands free, he took the ring from his mouth and tried it on. It was a little snug, but he gave no fucks. Baylor wanted to marry him.

His throat suddenly swelled. Someone wanted to keep him. Forever. He couldn't breathe.

Baylor sat up and wrapped his arms around Chipper's waist. He buried his face against his stomach. "I know. Every day, I woke up with that same emptiness and took it to bed every night. I'll never let you feel that way again."

Baylor got him in a way no one else ever had. He held the back of Baylor's head. "I should've known you would be the one to ask and save me. You already shocked the hell out of me by telling me you love me first."

Baylor jerked back. "What?" He looked adorably outraged. "You said it first."

Chipper shook his head as he crawled onto the bed, forcing Baylor onto his back. "Nope. I yelled that I chose you because I decided at that moment to retire. You yelled back that you love me."

Baylor looked dumbfounded. "No." The horror in his voice was hilarious. "Go back in time and say it first. You're already too cocky."

Chipper snorted. He nuzzled Baylor's neck. "Nope. It's too late. You have to suck it up and live with it. I did all the psycho chasing.

You can handle being the first to admit this is love. It's only fair."

Baylor sniffed as obnoxiously as possible. "I suppose I can handle people hearing I was first, as long as they also know you kidnapped me."

Chipper laughed so hard, no sound emerged. He kissed Baylor's neck. "He loveeees me," Chipper sang, teasing him.

Baylor cupped his head and lifted his hips as if seeking relief. "He really does."

The mood changed. Chipper kissed a path down Baylor's body while tearing open the front of his jeans. He needed Baylor's dick in his mouth. Chipper barely set Baylor's erection free before he swallowed it. This man intended to marry Chipper. Chipper would never let him regret it. He followed the sounds Baylor made, giving him all the pleasure he could want. Chipper also used the distraction to peel the pants off his body. He felt around blindly for the lube. Between the lube and his spit, he got Baylor as wet as possible. He fingered him, stretching and toying with the hot button he knew Baylor loved. The moment Baylor tensed, Chipper shot upward and shoved his way inside. He had to feel Baylor's orgasm on his dick. Chipper finished him with his hand and savored the sensation of Baylor's body milking him. This body now belonged to him. He was scared as hell to watch this slip away. Chipper was completely in his feelings as he pumped inside Baylor.

"Blow for me, sexy. Fill me with cum. You're so fucking hot when you come."

He was so close. Chipper had to taste Baylor's tongue. He sucked it as his body tensed. He strained so hard, he expected his mind to snap. Instead, he saw the future as so much ecstasy raced through him he nearly passed out. They would have a beautiful life. A wedding and kids. Chipper thought he would make an amazing stay-at-home dad while Baylor kept his business going...at a much slower pace. They would travel the world. Chipper would homeschool so they were never trapped to a schedule. The desperation he felt for that life was next level. He couldn't stop kissing Baylor and trying to will it all to be true.

Cum leaked from Baylor as Chipper pulled out. He had gotten carried away and forgotten a condom. Baylor had begged for his cum, so he wouldn't sweat it. Not to mention, they'd had the whole been tested conversation already. And they were getting fucking married. He wanted to scream it from the rooftops.

"I'll have a family." Even Chipper heard the wonder in his voice.

"Me too."

Until Baylor said the words, he hadn't fully considered that aspect. He didn't know why he hadn't thought about what Baylor would gain. Maybe he had been too focused on what Baylor had lost. Either way, they would fill each other's lives with love.

Chipper rolled to his side and pulled Baylor as close as possible, snuggling him.

"Zander has close ties to some sort of adoption agency. It deals in kids coming from the worst circumstances—like Rhorey. In fact, that's how Corey and Rhett ended up with him. Maybe, when you're ready, we can—"

Chipper found himself underneath Baylor. Baylor's tongue fought with his. By the time Baylor pulled away, Chipper felt like he had run a marathon. His chest heaved, fighting for breath through the love and lust.

Baylor rested his forehead against Chipper's. He stared into Chipper's eyes. "You're perfect. I'd love to fill our house with kids. But maybe let's wait until we've had a little time alone."

Chipper squeezed Baylor's ass. "All right. I do like having you alone."

Baylor sat back on his heels and peeled off his shirt, making Chipper realize he still wore half his clothes. He had been beyond desperate to get inside Baylor.

"You always have me rushing to have you. One of these days, I might get to make love to you slowly, torturing you."

Baylor settled on his chest. "Maybe. I mean, we have the rest of our lives. It has to happen eventually, right?"

Damn. They really did. Chipper would get to love Baylor in every way he ever fantasized.

He would get to hold him every night. "I can't wait to marry you."

Baylor's sexy green eyes flipped upward and met his stare. "Same."

They shared a heated look. Before meeting Baylor, he hadn't realized people just knew when they met their other half. There was no doubt. Every moment together felt comfortable and right—like they had known each other forever. He had zero doubt it would always be this way between them. Chipper would hold Baylor just like this for the rest of his life. They would talk about their day. Share their dreams and then help each other achieve them. Chipper knew now what he had been missing his entire life. Now that he found it, Chipper would never let Baylor go.

Chapter Eleven

BAYLOR HAD PLANNED THOUSANDS of weddings. Putting one together with Chipper was an adventure. Chipper had... ideas. They all made Baylor laugh. Sometimes, he let Chipper win. He had already agreed to hire a tattoo artist for the reception and set up a bouncy castle. They would also have lawn games along with an adult ball pit. Baylor knew Chipper had a childlike personality. A carnival-style wedding fit him perfectly. Plus, Chipper would never do anything like everyone else. He wanted their wedding to stand out in people's memories. Baylor wanted that too, but he had only given in to the tattoo artist when Chipper said he wanted to be the one to get the first one that day: Baylor's name along with their wedding date. Chipper kept him smiling.

Zander had offered his enormous compound of a house as a venue. Baylor spent way too much time invading the man's home, trying to figure out logistics. Narrowing down the guest list would be the death of him. He wanted all their friends to come. Baylor equally wanted to keep it reasonable. It was Zander's home, after all. He didn't want the place to be overrun. Plus, Zander planned to provide security. He knew Zander could afford it, but he still hoped to keep that expense down as much as possible. Baylor also prayed the weather cooperated for the day. He planned to keep everyone outside. Zander's backyard was the perfect size, and it faced the beach. The pictures would be top tier. Baylor focused on everything under the sun to keep himself sane. His nerves were bad, but the excitement also had him ready to scream. Baylor wanted to be married right now. Nothing happened fast enough for him.

After walking the property for the thousandth time, he went in search of his sexy, soon-to-be husband. He found him where he always did, competing against Zander's guards at their indoor obstacle course. Shirtless, climbing the rock wall, muscles flexed, making Baylor weak. He chewed his thumbnail and ate up the sight of Chipper's perfect body showing out in a powerful display of strength. Baylor was half a second away from moaning when Chipper reached the top, turned and spotted him. His immediate bright smile made Baylor's breath catch. Love poured through him.

Chipper motioned for Baylor to join him.

Baylor snorted. He had to shout to be heard over the sound of rushing water. "There's no way in hell I'm making it up there."

"You can do it. I believe in you."

Baylor thought there was a chance he could do it, but he didn't want to humiliate himself if he failed. Even having left his shoes in the mudroom, he wasn't dressed for wall climbing. "I don't have anything to wear after I get wet." There was definitely no way he could climb a waterfall rock formation and stay dry.

A squeal burst from Baylor when his feet suddenly left the ground. He found himself over a huge shoulder, holding on for dear life, and headed up the wall at an inhuman speed. He covered his eyes as the shallow pool of water at the bottom got farther away. Then he was on his feet at the top.

Zander's guard, Pytor, smiled like an idiot at his shock.

"There. You can enjoy the view." His thick Russian accent didn't show even a hint of guilt. In fact, it was obvious he fought a laugh.

Baylor peeked over the edge. It honestly wasn't that high, but he still discovered a new and horrible fear of heights. "Holy shit. How am I supposed to get back down?"

Chipper physically turned Baylor's body. On the other side of the waterfall, a slide for the indoor pool waited.

"I'm fully dressed—like phone, wallet, and all."

"Oops." Chipper didn't sound like he felt the least bit guilty.

"Toss your stuff down. I'll catch it."

At the shouted words, Baylor glanced down again. A guy he had never seen before waited in the pool below. He might have been a stranger, but the alternative was having his shit ruined. He tossed the items from his pockets down one at a time. The guy set everything on the edge of the pool.

"Thanks."

He got a thumbs-up in response.

"Come on." Chipper took his hand. "We'll go down together."

Suddenly, Baylor felt younger than he had in years. That was one of the many things Baylor found irresistible about Chipper. He breathed life and happiness back into Baylor. Not only had he lost that before him, Baylor hadn't expected he would ever feel this way again.

Baylor plopped down into the water at the top of the slide, soaking his pants. Chipper sat down behind him and wrapped his arms around Baylor. Baylor smiled like an idiot when Chipper pushed, sending them careening down the slide. A laugh burst from him a half second before the water engulfed him. He swiped his hair back as he broke the water's surface. His cheeks ached from the huge grin he wore. He wrapped his legs and arms around Chipper, holding on like a monkey while Chipper kept them afloat.

The guy who caught his stuff swam their way. "Hey. You must be the Baylor I've been hearing all about. We keep missing each other every time you've been here."

Baylor nodded. He held out a hand over Chipper's shoulder. "Nice to meet you."

The guy shook. "You too. I'm Legend, Pytor and Yaro's husband." Legend said the words, looking exactly like a man who expected to get judged.

Two husbands. Fuck. He could see it, though. The three fit. They were all gigantic and nice. Baylor never stopped smiling. He would never judge anyone for finding a slice of happiness in a world that actively tried killing everyone every day. "You must be amazing, then. Pytor and Yaro are great guys."

Legend's smile lost its brittle edge. "They really are."

As if hearing his cue, Pytor made a gigantic splash, cannon-balling into the water. Yaro came down the slide, holding a small bundle. A child's wild, happy scream cut through the air. When he came up laughing, Baylor realized it was Rhorey.

"Hey!" Baylor was ridiculously happy to see him. "It's my favorite pilot."

He swam Baylor's way, smiling. "Hi."

Baylor reached out and gave Rhorey something to latch onto. When he grabbed Baylor's arm, Baylor towed him in, forcing Chipper to hold everyone's weight. As far as Baylor knew, Rhorey had never acknowledged Chipper. With Baylor there, he obviously felt safe. That warmed Baylor's heart.

"Hey, buddy."

Rhorey didn't stop smiling at Chipper's greeting. "I went down the big slide!"

"I saw. You were very brave. That's a tall slide. It took me ages to go down it."

Baylor looked between them. Feelings swelled in his chest. He suddenly wanted a huge family with Chipper with the power of a nuclear bomb. Sooner rather than later. Chipper would be an amazing dad. He was such a big kid.

"I like heights. I'm going to fly planes. Uncle Zander says he'll make sure I get all the right certifications and then I can fly their missions to help save kids just like me. I can work for the family."

"Whoa. Hey, little dude. Do you want to go down again?"

At Yaro's question, Rhorey launched himself at the giant guard. They swam away, leaving Baylor staring after them and wondering what the hell Rhorey meant.

Chipper kissed his ear, distracting him. "You're such a sexy dad."

Baylor's eyelids dropped at the sensation of Chipper's lips on his skin. "Funny. I just had the same thoughts about you."

Chipper's lips moved to Baylor's neck. "I don't think we have the patience to wait as long as you think."

Baylor lost track of the conversation. All he felt was Chipper's body against his. "Wait for what? To get married or for us to have kids?"

"Both." Chipper nibbled his neck.

"Jesus. You're killing me and we are *not* alone."

Chipper chuckled against his skin. "I can't help it. You just do it for me and I'm dying. It's been six months. How much longer until this wedding already?"

Damn. They had planned to wait a year to give them time to properly plan. Baylor regretted that choice a little more every day. He ran his hands across Chipper's sexy, solid shoulders. With Chipper's mouth on his skin, Baylor realized how badly he didn't want to wait. "I mean, I have everything planned out. If we spent the week calling vendors and guests, we could be ready by next weekend."

"I get to carry rings next weekend?" The excited little voice that silently appeared had Chipper laughing in triumph.

Baylor dropped his forehead to Chipper's shoulder. Chipper knew Baylor couldn't say no to Rhorey.

He blew out a breath before looking Rhorey's way. "If your dads are okay with making the trip again next weekend, then yes. If they can't make it, we'll wait until you can be here."

A huge grin met his words.

Rhorey dog-paddled his way back toward the throuple who were obviously his babysitters for the day. "I get to carry rings next weekend!"

Chipper kissed his ear, chuckling. "That boy really loves you."

Baylor thought it was more a case of Rhorey having a heart of gold. "The feeling is mutual. He's an amazing kid."

Chipper kept trying to seduce him as if they didn't have an audience. "He'll be a great cousin to our kids."

Baylor closed his eyes and melted into Chipper's touch. The next week would be a nightmare of scrambling. Chipper was worth every second. He was worth everything.

Keep an eye out for the next Sporting Pride, *Dead Ball Situation*.

Content

THIS BOOK DEALS WITH abuse, death, and grieving.

About the Author

CHARITY PARKERSON IS AN award-winning and multi-published author with several companies. Born with no filter from her brain to her mouth, she decided to take this odd quirk and insert it in her characters. One of her greatest loves is writing morally gray characters. You'll find them scattered throughout her hundreds of titles.

*Nine-time Readers' Favorite Award Winner

*2015 Passionate Plume Award Finalist

*2013 Reviewers' Choice Award Winner

*2012 ARRA Finalist for Favorite Paranormal Romance

*Five-time winner of The Mistress of the Darkpath

Connect with her online:

*Sign up for her newsletter: https://bit.ly/charityparkersonnewsletter

*Join her readers' group on Facebook: http://bit.ly/CharitysTribe

* Website : https://www.charityparkerson.com

*A list of her social media accounts and giveaways all in one place: http://hy.page/charityparkerson

www.ingramcontent.com/pod-product-compliance
Lightning Source LLC
Chambersburg PA
CBHW060913250626
47159CB00008B/2992